The Pure:
Book Three of the Oz Chronicles

by

R.W. Ridley

I0571772

Single 'R' Imprint
Middlebury House Publishing,
Printed in USA

The Pure

DEDICATION:

As always For Mom, Dad, and Marianna

ACKNOWLEDGMENTS:

No one writes in a vacuum. I truly appreciate the support and input from all my friends, family, the good people of Tullahoma, TN, and the fans of Book One and Book Two. I hope Book Three lives up to your expectations.

R.W. Ridley

The Pure: Book Three of The Oz Chronicles

ONE

The dead watch me when I sleep. As you can imagine, I don't get a lot of sleep.

I don't know what they want with me, but the hate in their lifeless eyes doesn't suggest they want to throw me a party.

"There's all kinds of dead in the Délon's world." That's what my best friend, Gordy Flynn, told me right before his dead sister tried to have me as an after-life snack. Then again, it's possible that didn't happen at all. It's possible I imagined the whole thing. Even Gordy. I don't know anymore.

My room is dark. Even in the daytime. A single fluorescent light flickers above my head. It gives off the illusion that the walls are breathing. At least I hope it's an illusion. I don't have a view of the outside world. I can't recall ever seeing it since I've been in this... "facility." I'm not even sure what kind of "facility" it is. Judging by the crazy people that walk the halls, I'm guessing it's a loony bin, but I don't want to think that because it will mean I'm one of the crazies.

The things in my mind, the things I see and remember, I should think I'm crazy, but I can't quite let myself believe it. Maybe that's what a crazy person would believe. Canter, the half-crab, half-man freak that visits me every night, wants me to believe I'm crazy. I don't know why, because if I'm crazy, he's just a figment of my imagination, and he doesn't really exist.

I hear the locks on my door slide back, and the door opens. Chester, the giant orderly steps inside. "You ready, little man?"

I sit on my bed, exhausted from watching the dead watch me all night. "Don't call me that."

"What should I call you?" Chester snickers.

"My name's Oz."

"All right, Oz, you ready? Doc's on a tight schedule."

I don't stand right away. I'm testing him. "What is a DH?"

"A what?"

"A DH. I overheard the pharmacist call me a DH."

He steps farther into the room. He lowers his head and peers down at me. "You don't need to concern yourself with that. Now, c'mon. Let's go."

I fold my arms over my chest. "What is it?"

He sighs and rubs one of his giant hands on the back of his neck. "You're killing me, little man... Oz."

"Tell me, and I'll go with you."

He chuckles. "You're coming with me no matter what." "Not without a fight. I'll go willingly if you tell me."

He thinks it over. "I ain't in the mood for no fight today."

He looks over his shoulder to make sure nobody is within earshot.

Back to me. "Double homicide."

"What?"

"DH stands for double homicide."

I can feel the blood rush to my cheeks. I'm embarrassed, and I'm not sure that's the proper reaction. I should be angry. "I don't like that."

"You asked," Chester says. "Now get up, or Dr. Graham is going to sick a skinner on me."

I cock my head. Did I hear what I think I heard? "A what?"

"Get up!" he barks.

"What did you just say?" I bark back.

"I said get up, or Dr. Graham is going to skin me alive." He grabs my arm and yanks me to my feet.

"You said 'skinner.'" I say dragging my feet as he forces me to the door.

"I said no such thing because I don't know what in tarnation a skinner is. You're hearing things." He tosses me in the hallway. "You broke your word. You said if I told you what DH meant you wouldn't put up a fight. You're fighting me like a cat going in a bag."

"You said skinner."

"Fine," Chester says. "If it will make you feel better I said skinner."

It doesn't make me feel better.

The hallway is lined with crazies. Some crazier than others. A short man with saggy jowls compulsively sticks his dentures out of his mouth and sucks them back in over and over again. He has a vacant look in his eyes.

A fat woman with a see-through hairdo farts, and the sound scares her as if someone had just snuck up behind her and screamed "boo" in her ear.

We turn the corner following the yellow line on the floor. Ahead of us to the right, leaning against a door jamb, is a man with no eyes or nose. His face looks as though it has been scooped out. I stare in disgusted awe.

"Stop eyeballing me, boy," Scoop-face demands.

How did he know?

3

"Relax, Mr. Maynard," Chester says. "Don't nobody want to look at your ugly face."

Scoop-face chuckles. "The uglier you are the more people stare. You ought to know that, Chester." He laughs revealing his toothless mouth. "Where you taking the young crazy?"

I am struck by his use of the word 'young.' According to Dr. Graham, I'm forty years old. The same age I imagine Scoop-face is. Although, it's hard to tell. But then again, he can't even see me. Can he?

"Dr. Graham's. And you need to get your eyes checked. This crazy ain't but a few years younger than you."

"Ha-ha," Scoop-face replies sarcastically. "Ain't nothing wrong with my eyes." He sticks out his slimy tongue, flicking it like a snake. Drool forms on his chin. He slurps it back in his mouth. "You're crazy, don't taste no older than a boy. Fourteen or fifteen, I'd say."

We pass the poor disfigured soul. Chester is half-dragging me as I look at the man in total amazement.

"Say something, young crazy," Scoop-face barks. "Let me hear you talk."

I say the first thing that comes to my mind. "What happened to your face?"

He hesitates. If he had eyes they would have been wide open. He is surprised by my voice. "It's you."

Chester tosses me ahead of him. "You're wearing on my last nerve, Oz. Get it in gear or I'm going to put you in restraints."

The threat is enough to get me to change my attitude quickly. I have experienced the restraints before. I don't know why or when, but I have a vivid memory of the fear and pain. I know I never want to experience that again.

I feel the eyeless stare of Scoop-face as we turn the corner.

***

Dr. Graham is annoyed by me today. I haven't done anything, but his impatience for my mere existence is obvious in the way he sits in his chair. He purses his lips together as he taps his Bic pen on a small yellow notepad in his lap.

"That's weird," I say.

The doctor stops tapping the pen. "What's weird?"

"I never thought of it before." I stare at the pen.

He twirls his penned hand signaling me to elaborate. "You're using a pen... and paper."

"I often do when I want to write something down," the doctor says.

I scratch my head. "But this is... the 2030s, I would think we'd have come up with something better by now. More high tech."

The doctor smiles. "If it makes you feel any better, the pen does have a nice cushiony easy grip."

I look at his clothes. "Styles haven't changed much in 30 years."

He looks down at his coat. "It's hard to improve on the white lab coat." He writes something on the yellow pad. "What year would you like it to be, Oz?" A smirk forms on his face.

I watch him write. Ignoring his question I say, "I didn't kill anyone."

He stops writing and looks at me, right eyebrow raised, lips taut.

"I know that's what you want me to believe..."

"I want you to get better, Oz. I'm afraid that may mean you facing some uncomfortable truths." His posture changes. He's gone from irritated to confused. He doesn't know what to do next.

"How did I do it?" The words come out of my mouth with little thought. I am instantly sorry I asked the question. I pray he won't answer.

"You tell me," he says. He is studying me. This is some game they teach you in shrink school. If I play, he wins.

I twist in my chair and face the opposite wall.

"Very well, Oz." He clears his throat. "New topic. Do you know a woman by the name of Millie B. Story?"

"No." I answer with my back still to him.

"She's written me," the doctor says.

"Congratulations."

"She wants permission to visit with you."

I slowly turn toward him. I run the name over and over again in my head. I can't place it. "Why?"

When a shrink asks you a question, even if it's the simplest question in the world, you have to measure your response carefully. He cares more about how you answer than what you answer. He is mining your face, your body, your tone for the secret to who you really are. The truth is I didn't know who I was, and I didn't want the doc finding out before me.

"I don't know her," I say, coating every inch of my response in disinterest. In point of fact, I am dying to know who she is. "But if she wants to visit me, let her visit me. What do I care?"

I can see the gears turning in the doc's head. "I'll give it some thought." He returns to tapping his pen on the yellow notepad. "We should return to last week's session."

"What about it?"

"Some things remain unanswered," he says as he flips through his notebook. "The Source, for one." He clears his throat. "We still don't know where or what it is."

"Does it matter?"

He looks surprised. "I believe it does. It's the key to you getting better. I'm sure of it."

"I'm not so sure." I look at my hands. They are unnaturally old. "It's just crazy talk."

He shakes his head. "We don't like that word, Oz."

"What word?"

"Crazy. Crazy is used by people who don't understand how the mind works."

I snicker. "Then it's okay for me to use it because I don't understand how the mind works."

"Nevertheless, I'd prefer if we steer clear of that word." He is stern but sympathetic.

I shrug my shoulders.

He looks back at his notepad. "You know..." he says as he jots something down in the margins of the pad. "You mentioned that there were nine dogs."

"Yeah," I say impatiently.

"Well, all but Kimball seem to be missing from the end of your last story." He flips through the pages. "Yes, yes, Kimball is with Wes and the others, but you don't mention the other dogs."

I run the story over in my head. "Oh... hmmmm. I don't know. Is that important?"

The doc taps his pen on the notepad. "I'm not sure. I just find it puzzling."

I share his bewilderment. I had not given those other dogs a second thought until now. They just disappeared. Perhaps my twisted imagination was running dry.

Doctor Graham stands unexpectedly. The act of it startles me. His hands fall to his waist, right hand holding the notepad, the left holding the pen. I scan them quickly.

Just a week ago, he had a purple rash. No signs of it now.

"Perhaps, we should try another regression." He motions for me to enter the back part of his office. I look past him and stare at the couch. My throat goes dry. I can hear the blood rushing through my head. I am glued to my chair.

"Oz?" he says.

I am frozen. The sound of the metronome hits me for the first time. Has it been going the whole time?

"I..." My palms start to sweat. I look up at him. "Not today, Doc." The room starts to spin.

When Doctor Graham talks, he sounds a million miles away. "The Pure won't be happy."

The room starts to vibrate. I feel a thump in my throat. I think it's clogging my ears. It sounded like the doc just said something about the Pure. "Oz," his voice is now strikingly clear. "It's purely up to you. I'm not going to force you to do anything you don't want to."

I shake my head and blow out a big puff of air. "I want to go back to my room. Can I?" It feels strange for me to call it "my room." Part of me finds the phrase completely foreign although I know I have spoken it before.

"Of course," Doctor Graham taps a silver bell on his desk. It lets out a high-pitched tone that screeches through the room. It's oddly low-tech. Just one more thing that doesn't fit.

Chester enters the room. "Trouble?"

"No..." the doctor looks at me with a sympathy I did not think he was capable of. "No, not at all. Oz isn't feeling well. Can you escort him back to his room?" He turns to walk to his desk, but then stops. "Have Nurse Kline put Mr. Griffin on her rounds tonight. I want her looking in on him every hour." He addresses me with a loud and deliberate tone. "Just as a precaution, Oz. For your own good."

I am too disoriented to argue. Besides, maybe she'll keep the dead away.

***

I spend the journey back to the room wondering why the doc asked me about the dogs. It seems to be a ridiculously unimportant point. There are so many other things he could ask me about.

As I walk through the hallway with Chester's meaty hand wrapped around my upper arm, I begin to wonder myself what happened to the dogs.

"Snarkel, snapper, momma, jaws!" a young kid shouts from the doorway of his room. "Snarkel, snapper, momma, jaws spot, jumper," he says with a grin. He's obviously very happy that he's caught my attention. The young man is emaciated. His elbows look sharp as knives and his cheekbones look like small mountains on his otherwise sunken face. "Hambone, Charlie boy."

I smile politely and nod.

He winks. "It's a secret code."

"It's crazy code," Chester laughs.

"Dr. Graham doesn't like that word," I say, eyes shifting upward as Chester tightens his grip on my arm.

"Yeah?" Chester says. "I don't like taxes, but I still gotta pay 'em... most of them... some of them." He turns to the skinny young man and shoots him a menacing glare. "Back in your room, Bones. Don't nobody want to hear your code today."

Bones backs up. "Snarkel's going to get you. You'll see."

Chester raises a brawny fist as we continue down the hall. "I got something for Snarkel when he comes to get me." He laughs loudly and alone.

We turn the corner. Scoop-face's room is just ahead. I am relieved that he is not there. Beyond his disfigurement, or maybe because of the enormity of it, I am deeply unsettled by him. He seems to have an eerie peace about his... affliction. I can understand a man adjusting to the loss of an arm or a leg. There are prosthetics to help you cope, to simulate the missing extremity and a passable number of functions it once served. But to lose a face? There is no prosthetic to replace that. None that I had ever heard of, anyway.

We round another corner and reach my room. Chester pushes me inside. He pulls the door shut quickly and punches in a code on the keypad next to the door. I hear the lock tumble and click into place. He looks through the eight-inch square window and sprouts a vindictive little grin. "Good night," his muffled voice cracks. "Don't let the shunters bite."

I stop mid breath as I'm exhaling and scan his grinning face. Did he just say shunter? I step toward the door with my eyes fixed on his mouth.

He nods. "What?" He doesn't like my expression.

"Say it again," I say, just shy of demanding.

He shakes his head. "You really are the lunatic fringe, little man." With that, he moves away from the small window and moves down the hall.

***

The next face I see in the small window is Nurse Kline's. An hour earlier I cried myself to sleep. My mind collapsed in on itself. I had never felt more out of place in my entire life. At least, I think I hadn't. As I was breaking

10

down, I felt as if I had done it before, many times before, yet I had no memory of it. The feeling of it was new and frighteningly painful.

My eyes closed, and my brain almost completely shut down, I begin to feel the movement around me. They're here. The dead. Crawling, walking, zooming all around me. I can smell them. I am afraid to open my eyes. One tugs at my sheet. Another one runs its clammy fingers through my hair.

"Osmond," one whispers.

Another one gargles something incoherent yet terrifying. The tone of its voice is set in a level of anger I can't even begin to imagine.

Finally, it is too much for me to bear. I open my eyes and back against the corner of the iron headboard that meets the wall. I am breathing so erratically, I am almost hyperventilating. The room is dim, illuminated by the sparse light poking through the window on the door. I see the figure of a pale child scamper across the room, his bare feet slapping against the cold concrete floor. He turns to me just before he disappears into the darkest corner. His face is rotted. Worms crawl from his exposed cheekbone. His nose is hanging by a flap of skin. I scream at the sight of it. He vanishes into the darkness.

"They don't like you."

The man's voice comes from my right. I am too startled to scream or shout for help. I manage to say "Wha...," but nothing more.

"Relax," the voice continues.

"Who's there?" I search through the grayness of the room. In the corner across from where the dead boy disappeared, I spot him, Scoop-face.

"It's just me," he says.

Somehow the knowledge that it is just him does not relax me. "Do you know how long I've been looking for you?" He steps toward me. He moves like a man who can see.

"No," I answer.

"A long friggin' time." He laughs. "'Cept in my case, it ain't so much looking as it is searching." He points to the vacant area on his face.

"Do I know you?"

He sits on the edge of the bed. I move as far away from him as possible. "Used to... I think."

"How did you get in here?"

He tugs on his left ear. "I heard Chester punching in the code to your door this evening. I got ears like a dog now that my face is gone. I can pretty much hear anything."

"How..."

"How did I get this hole in my face?" He chuckled. "You know what they say." He leans in closer. "Don't ever try to remove a shunter from the host's face." He laughs and a wad of spit drips out of his mouth and rests on his chin.

I don't react. My mind has been playing tricks on me all day. He didn't say shunter. I wasn't going to fall for that again. I was tired of being my demented brain's whipping boy.

"You ain't got nothing to say?" He cocks his head. If he had eyes, I would no doubt see a puzzled look on his face.

"What's to say?"

"Hell, boy, I just confirmed what's been whirling around in that pointy head of yours. This ain't no hospital. They's inside of you." He reaches out and cups the top of my head with his thick hand. "They's crawling around in there, 'tween the grooves in that squishy brain of yours, and they's trying to find what they ain't got."

I knock his hand away. "Oh, what's that?"

"The Source."

I swallow hard. "This is a trick. You're crazy. We're both crazy."

Scoop-face thinks it over. "Well, hell, yeah I'm crazy. I had my eyes ripped out, and my nose tore off by some slimy little face sucker with about a thousand tentacles, and I lived to tell about it. That'd make anyone crazy." He laughs and chokes on a wad of mucus stuck in this throat. He hacks and coughs so loud I wait for nurse Kline to appear at the window, but she doesn't come. He catches his breath and wheezes, "We're all crazy, kid. You, me, and everyone whatever survived the end of the world."

I scoot to the end of the bed. "The world didn't end," I say as I stand.

"Don't do that."

"What?"

"Stand. Move around. My quilibrium's all shot. I get nauseous if people move around."

"Quilibrium? You mean equilibrium?"

"Whatever the damn word is, I ain't got none of it." He sounds angry for the first time. "Now sit"

I comply although I'm not sure why.

"The Délons is real. The Takers is real. The Silencers is real." He leans in and whispers. "The Pure is real."

I start to sway. I desperately want him to shut up.

"You got to snap out of this fool business here. This is the part that ain't real."

I feel a pressure in my throat and chest. It's panic. I will burst into tears soon. I have done this before. Many times before. I whimper.

"Don't you do that," Scoop-face insists. "Don't you set off to your balling again."

"Again?" What does he mean?

"Yes, again. We go through this nonsense pert-near every night, and I'm worn to my last nerve. We are running out of time. You forget a little bit more every day."

Confused I say, "You said you've been searching for me for a long time. Now you say we've been through this before."

He shakes his faceless head. "We have, and we haven't. You got to stop thinking like that."

"Like what?"

"Like time ticks away on a clock. It don't. It jumps and stops and starts, goes all over the place. You do things for the first time over and over again."

"I don't know what to believe."

"The purple dead-eyed pigs whittle away everything you got in here," he points to his head. "'til there ain't nothing left, but the Source."

"I don't know what the Source is!" I scream and the tears follow a snot bubble shooting out of my nose.

"How do you know?"

"Because," I chuckle madly, "I know what I know."

He chuckles back. "Not for a long time, little Oz. Not for a long time."

"Leave," I demand.

He sighs in frustration. "Do me a favor."

"Why?"

"Because I'm an old-fart without a face. Life ain't been exactly Santa Claus to me. The least you can do for me is one stinkin' favor."

I mull it over. There is a long penetrating silence between us. Finally, I say, "What?"

"Ask Doc Graham for a GP pass tomorrow."

"A what?"

14

"A general population pass."

"Why?"

"Just do it."

Without turning toward him I say, "What makes you think he'll give me one?"

"Cause they're getting impatient. They've drilled and drilled and drilled into that little pea brain of yours, and they ain't come no closer to finding the Source than the day they started this whole mess."

I clear my throat. "Will you leave if I agree?"

"That hurts my heart, kiddo. You and me are friends from way back, and this is the thanks I get." He stands. "I'll leave if you agree."

"I'll ask for a GP pass."

He shuffles toward the door, talking as he walks. "There's a janitor's closet three doors down from the doc's office."

"What of it?"

"Be in it at 11:00 tomorrow."

"What for?"

He stops and grins, "Because Lou wants to say 'Hi'."

TWO

The dead do not leave until morning. I have not slept for longer than a ten minute stretch in... years. I cannot remember a time when I was not tired. I cannot remember a time when I was not scared. I cannot remember a time... clearly. That's the problem. If I am the age Dr. Graham says I am, I have lived an entire life without one single shred of a memory to hold onto. It doesn't seem possible.

Yet believing that I battled an army of slobbering, greasy monsters and purple dead-eyed freaks seems even more preposterous. I am crazy. I am insane. I am out of my ever-loving mind.

For all I know, nothing is real. I am neither who Dr. Graham says I am nor who Scoop-face says I am. I am a dream. A twisted, grotesque nightmare inside the head of some bratty kid who watches too many scary movies or plays too many zombie video games. I will be gone as soon as he wakes up. God, how I wish he would wake up.

I lie in bed and do not move. I stare at the ceiling... through the ceiling, really. If I stare hard enough, maybe I can see the beady little eyes of the spoiled turd who is making me live this horrible nightmare.

The familiar tone of numbers being punched on the door's keypad diverts my attention from the ceiling. Nurse Kline enters carrying a tray of food.

"Breakfast is served," she says setting the tray down on a table near the bed.

I stare at the oatmeal in a plastic bowl.

"You best eat up."

I look at her. My eyes burn from lack of sleep. "Do I like oatmeal?"

She smiles. "Don't you know?"

"I don't know anything."

"You love it." She walks back to the door. "I'll bring you some juice if you want."

I shake my head. "I want to see Dr. Graham."

She shakes her head and considers my request. "You're not on the schedule today."

"I don't care."

"You might not, but his other patients..."

"I want to see Dr. Graham. He's my doctor. I want to see him." I am much more abrupt with her than I'd intended.

She considers arguing but, to her credit, doesn't. "I'll see what I can arrange."

"Now!" I bark.

Her jaw sets as she mashes her teeth together. She wants to let me have it with both barrels, but she backs off. "Very well."

She shuts the door. The lock tumbles into place. I hear the muffled sounds of a conversation. It's heated. Chester's face appears in the window. I have never seen him with such a serious expression. He grunts and moves down the hallway.

I lie back down and stare at the ceiling again. The patterns in the tile begin to take on shapes: a cat, a tree, a bus. A scene begins to form in my head, a thought, a memory.

I'm on Westwood Avenue in Tullahoma. The dogwoods are in bloom. The smell of honeysuckle is in the air. Hummingbirds feed on a nearby bush. The sound of their wings ripping through the wind is deafening. I sprint out of earshot of the tiny little noisemakers. Ahead I see Gordy. A young spry Gordy. He's no older than six. He's talking to another boy. I dig my feet into the ground as I pump my legs faster and faster to reach them.

I get to my old friend and quickly identify the other boy, Stevie Dayton. His eyes are puffy slits. Gordy is laughing.

"Look at the retard cry! Look at the little retard baby!"

"What..." I want to ask what's going on, but the words aren't coming out. I walk up to Stevie and slap him across the face. What am I doing?

"Little retard! Little retard!" I hear the words come out of my mouth. Stop! Stop! My mind is about to explode. I can't be doing this. I'm not doing this.

"Punch him, Oz," Gordy says. He scans the immediate area. "Ain't nobody around."

I can feel myself hesitate.

"Do it, chicken head! Do it!" Gordy is bouncing up and down in an uncontrolled fury. "Punch the cry baby retard!"

I watch in horror as my fist flies forward and lands squarely on Stevie's nose. Oh, God no. No, no, no. Stevie, I'm so sorry. I'm so sorry...

Blood drips from Stevie's fat nose. Tears well up in his eyes. He cups his hands over his face, but he doesn't run. He looks at me. "It's o'day, Oz. I see you in dere. It's o'day."

"Hit him again, Oz!"

"You see what in where?" I ask Stevie. I ask, but I know the answer. He sees me. Not the bully pounding him in the face, but me, the guy who so desperately wants to take back everything I did to him. The guy who wants to be Stevie's hero.

"I see it," he says.

I pound him in the nose again. "You see what?"

He's terrified, but still he doesn't run. "I see," he says between breaths. "I see da magic in you."

***

The door to my room opens and Dr. Graham enters. I am still caught up in my vivid memory or hallucination or whatever it is. I do not acknowledge the doctor.

"Oz?"

I am stuck... in those words... "da magic in you." What did Stevie mean?

"Oz, I don't have time..."

"Pass," I snap.

"What?"

"A GP pass. I want a GP pass." I turn to him, eyes still glazed.

He clears his throat and turns to Chester. I have never asked for this before. I can tell by their expressions that they don't know what to make of it.

"May I ask why?"

"I... I'm tired of this room."

He nods. "Understandable, but still. You've been reluctant to venture outside this room ever since you arrived."

"People change."

He purses his lips together and rubs his chin with his thumb. "Alright. I'll give you a restricted pass. You're not to go off the yellow path. Understood?"

"The yellow path. Right."

"This is a test, Oz. You play by the rules and do as I

say today, who knows what tomorrow will bring."

"Tomorrow. Got it."

"I'm not kidding," he says with a smile. "I'm cautiously optimistic about this request. It shows progress. Something you haven't shown before."

I smile this time. "Take a bow, Doc. You're a miracle worker. Next thing you know, I'll be running for president of the yellow path people."

***

What I soon come to find out is the yellow path people are really just a multitude of crazies who barely qualify to be human beings. They come in all shapes, sizes, colors, and ages. The only thing they have in common is the winding yellow line that divides the corridor floor throughout most of the hospital. There are other lines, red, green, blue, but I never see the people that inhabit those corridors. I see the occasional shadow of the blue crazies or red crazies or green crazies where the yellow line briefly dissects their paths, but I never get a close look.

A patient with leathery skin and walnut-sized lumps across his forehead stops me on my way to the janitor's closet.

"New?" he mumbles.

"I... I'm not sure," I answer

His stubbly chin quivers as he stutters "P-p-p-p-pudding." "What?"

"P-p-p..." He gulps to right himself. "Pudding to p—p-pass."

"Pudding?" I say as if this is a crazy request. Of course it's a crazy request. He's crazy. "I don't have pudding."

Upon hearing this, the leathery little man screams and rams his head into a nearby door jamb. The origin of his lumps suddenly becomes very clear. "Pudding to pass! Pudding to pass!"

As I stare at the man in disbelief, a bony hand appears in my field of vision holding a cup of chocolate pudding. Bones smiles back at me as I try to piece this scene together in my cluttered mind.

"It's his favorite," Bones says.

I don't respond. I'm seriously regretting my request for a GP pass.

"Take it. Give it to him. Before Chester comes."

I still hesitate. Bones slams his hand into my chest. I take the pudding and hand it to...

"Gator."

"What?"

Bones sighs in frustration. "His name's Gator. On account of his skin is all wrinkled and leathery. That's what they do in this place. They call you by what you look like instead of your real name. They call me..."

"Bones."

"That's right, Bones." He looks at Gator as he rips open the pudding cup. "He's harmless, 'cept to himself I suppose. He was a great man once... well, he claims he was anyway. I didn't know him 'fore they stuck me in here."

"Where is here?"

He looks around. "I don't really know. It's just here."

We begin to walk down the corridor. "Where do you come from?" I ask.

He thinks about the question. "I'm not sure. Still trying to figure that out." He leans in closer and whispers. "I'm your lookout."

"What?"

"Archie sent me."

"Archie?"

He reaches toward his face and mimics pulling it off. "Archie."

I nod. "Ahhh, yes, Archie. How come he has a name?"

He shrugs. "Guess don't nobody want to call him what he looks like." Bones scratches his head. "He says you're the key."

"I don't know what that means."

"Neither do I, but if Archie wants me to look out for you, that's what I aim to do. Won't nobody hurt you long as I'm around."

I look at his skinny frame and fight the urge to laugh at his bravado. He senses my skepticism. "Snarkel, snapper momma, jaws, spot, jumper, hambone, Charlie boy," he says with a smile. "Long as I got that, I'm friggin invincible. You understand?"

I don't have the heart to tell him "no" so I nod as if it makes perfect sense.

We reach the janitor's closet. We both stare at the door as if it might explode.

"No matter what you hear in there, don't come out," Bones says staring at the doorknob.

"What am I going to hear in there?"

"Don't know, but Gator was normal before he went in there." I look at him wide-eyed.

"Gator?"

He looks at me for a split second before he busts out laughing. "I'm just yanking your chain. Gator ain't never been in there... or normal, far as I know."

I look to my left and then to my right before putting my hand on the doorknob. Slowly I pull the door open and step inside the surprisingly roomy closet.

Bones gives me one last reassuring grin as the door slowly closes. "I got your back," he whispers. As the door clicks shut and I lose all light, I try to convince myself that it's reassuring to have Bones right outside the door.

I stand motionless, not knowing exactly what to expect or do. The sound of muffled voices comes from the back of the closet. I carefully step toward them. They are high up, toward the ceiling. My eyes adjust to the darkness , and I can make out a vent. The sounds of a conversation escape the metal grate.

The first voice I can make out is Dr. Graham's. "The other patients look up to you," he says.

"They're idiots," his companion answers back. "It's kind of like being looked up to by a pack of greasy rats. It don't mean much." I know by the comment more than the voice that it's Archie Scoop-face.

"You shouldn't dismiss the others so easily."

"Yeah, yeah, yeah. Yap, yap, yap. For a shrink you sure do talk a lot. Shouldn't you be listening?"

"Okay," the doc says sounding more than a little irritated. "Talk."

"Not here."

"What do you mean?"

"The couch. I want to go under."

There is an awkward silence.

"Hypnosis? Why?"

"What do you mean, why?" Scoop-face chuckles. "It's what you do, ain't it?"

"You called it a gallon of goose crap last week."

"Last week?" Scoop-face chuckles even louder. "You can't hold a crazy man's feet to the fire for a thing he said last week."

The doc clears his throat. "I don't like that word."

"I know... I had a change of heart, that's all. I got some

things I want to explore in the deep recesses of this dented head of mine. Now, are you going to help me or sit there with that puppy dog look on your face?"

I can hear movement. The doc shifts in his leather chair. I wonder how you hypnotize a man with no eyes. Are the eyes necessary? They aren't when you're under.

A chair squeaks. One of them clears his throat. "Very well," Dr. Graham says.

Silence. Then I hear the chairs being pushed back.

"Get your hands off me," Scoop-face snarls. "I know the daggum way."

Now I hear the shuffling of his feet. In my mind's eye, I see the doc nervously following him, watching him carefully, almost willing him to the couch without incident, one hand out to steady him if Scoop-face should happen to run into some errant piece of furniture.

Scoop-face can feel him there. He grunts in protest, but knows the doc doesn't mean anything by it. People do it to him all the time. They aren't as concerned about him as they are about themselves having to witness the possible catastrophe of a bumbling man with no face crashing to the floor.

I hear the swish of leather as Scoop-face's ass hits the couch. Dr. Graham adjusts his chair.

"Are you certain about this?" Dr. Graham asks.

"I'm on the couch, ain't I," Scoop-face answers. "Do your stuff, Doc."

I hear the soothing rhythm of the metronome begin. I breathe deeply as the soft ticking seeps in and fills the closet.

The doc pulls out his heavy monotone voice. "Listen to the sound of the metronome. Not just the sound it makes, but the sounds it doesn't make. Listen to the soft chorus of its entire existence, from sound to silence to sound and back to silence. Go beyond listening. Feel it now. Feel the gentle thumping in your chest. Feel the sound travel through your nerves and veins. Relax as it takes over your whole body. Relax. Getting sleepy now. Relax. Sleepier still. Relax."

He stops talking.

For several seconds there is nothing but the sound of the metronome.

Softly the doc says. "Where are you, Archie?"

"The woods. Running. Being chased."

"By who."

"Not who. What. Don't know." He screams suddenly. "What?" the doc asks sounding a little more panicked than I imagine he intends.

"They got Bobby! They got little Bobby!" His voice is cracking. Mucus is building up in this throat.

"Calm down, Archie. Calm down. Leave this place. Leave it now. Go somewhere safe. Find someplace safe…"

"Wait! They don't have him anymore. He got away. Somebody saved him. Somebody… It's…"

"Who, Archie? It's who?"

He sighs deeply. "Lou!"

Scoop-face

THREE

"You ain't never seen nothing like it. She can fight like nobody's business. Monster, man, or animal, she can hold her own with anything or anybody.

"Skinner dead. I see it now. That's who's chasing us through the woods. It's me, little Bobby Greeley, Tank Caldwell, and April Nelson. We're running for our friggin' lives. The skinner dead are organized now. They figured out they hunted better in packs than on their own. They hunt to eat , and they're always hungry.

"I still got my face at this point. I don't mind telling you, I'm a good-looking fella when I got my nose and eyes. I did all right with the ladies in my day, I tell you what, but that's the furthest thing from my simple little mind at the time. I'm just trying not to be food.

"Skinner dead ain't your typical zombies. They move different. I guess cause they been filleted by bugs they get bug ways in their bones. They can run like men and hop, crawl, and bite like bugs when they need to. The only thing we got going for us is they think like bugs, too. They ain't exactly splittin' the atom, if you know what I mean.

"One of the skinner dead, used to be an old lady it looks like, swoops down from a crooked oak and grabs up little Bobby. You ain't never heard a scream like that in all your life. The old lady, her fire-red inner flesh glistening, is cackling with joy because she caught some food. Bobby's screeching like a banshee. We all seen the skinner dead eat. It ain't pretty.

"Little Bobby, as you can imagine, ain't very big. He used to be a jockey when things was normal, before the end of the world. He used to be strong enough to manhandle a 1200 pound thoroughbred, but now he's small and puny. He couldn't walk a 20-pound dog without pulling his arm out of its socket. Doing nothing but surviving does that to a man. It cuts him down to a shell. The muscle and energy gives way to worry and fear. It just tears him down to nothing but a shadow of the man who used to live in its place.

"Anyway, there was little Bobby Greeley squirming under the hold of a skinner dead old lady. She's crowing and gnashing her teeth. She's got dinner. I feel terrible. There's nothing I can do because... well there ain't no way in hell I was going back to help him and become food myself. There's brave, and there's stupid, and I ain't neither.

"The skinner dead old lady sinks her teeth into Bobby's shoulder. He screams bloody murder. The other skinner dead are on their way to join in on the feast. Although, I can't imagine he'll be more than an appetizer to the group of... four or five.

"They were just twenty feet away or so when Lou swung out of the trees. She actually swung down on a vine like Tarzan. It was right out of the movies. She went feet first into the skinner dead old lady. Knocked the old hag into that crooked oak, snapped her ribs like matchsticks.

"But that kind of thing don't have much effect on the dead. The old lady leapt forward, little Bobby's flesh still stuck between her rotten teeth and tackled Lou to the ground. Lou stood and pulled a sword from a sheath around her waist. She swung, wildly at first, missing the old lady more than hitting her, but her frenzied ballet of slashes and grunts kept the other skinner dead at bay. They watched, clearly confused by the chaotic action, and waited for a lull in the combat to leap forward and take Lou down.

"She never gave them that lull. The old lady was cut to pieces and Lou advanced on the other skinner dead without missing a beat.

"'C'mon!' she screamed.

"'We's so hungry,' one of the skinner dead bellowed through shredded vocal chords. 'Please.'

"'The little one,' another one cried. 'That's all we need. We eats him up , and you go. We leave your yummy flesh be.'

"Me, Tank and April slowly move up and flank Lou. She turns and gives us a scolding stare. She wasn't happy we took so long to back her up.

"'Leave or I'll chop you to pieces like your friend here.'

"The skinner dead look at their fallen comrade. One scoops up a piece of the rotten skinless flesh and sniffs it. 'Bad, not for eats.'

"'Leave now,' Lou insisted.

"'Hungry,' the skinner dead closest to her said. It slowly crawls foreword.

"Lou stepped towards it. She let out a warrior cry like you've never heard. Ear piercing, frightening, thunderous. The skinner dead knew to the depths of their decaying bones that she was capable of anything, a kind of madness they could have never imagined.

"They huffed one by one and disappeared into the thick canopy of the forest. Their vanishing trick was unsettling. We sat in wait, sure that they would reappear as quickly as they'd disappeared, but as the minutes passed we realized they were really gone. Beaten back by one of the greatest warriors I have ever seen."

***

"'That was incredible.'

"We sat around a freshly built fire. April tended to little Bobby's wounded shoulder. Tank and I sat in awe of Lou as she cleaned her sword.

"I cleared my throat. 'I said that was incredible.'

"She snickered. 'You mean the way you deserted your buddy?'

"Tank, a thick hairy man in his twenties, held his big hands up to the fire. 'He was paying you a compliment... miss.'

"'Relax, Tank,' I said. 'She's right.'

"Flush faced, he turned to me prepared to defend his honor, but in the split second it took him to turn to me, he must have run the events over in his head and realized she was right. He simply nodded.

"'We ain't heros,' I said. 'Hell, a couple of years ago, I was in my first semester at a technical college in Birmingham. I was going to be an electrician. I didn't sign up for this.'

"She laughed. 'Nobody signed up for this, genius.'

"'You got a smart mouth on you,' Tank barked. 'What are you anyway, thirteen... fourteen?'

"She shrugged. 'Something like that,' she said examining the now shiny blade of her sword. 'I stopped counting a while back. Seemed pointless.'

"'Well, you're just a kid, anyhow,' Tank grunted. 'A little respect would be nice.'

"'Respect?' she laughed.

"'You alone?' I interrupted. Tank was about to start an argument he couldn't win. I didn't want to make an enemy of this girl.

"She stared at Tank. Disgust in her eyes. She was covered in mud and skinner dead blood, but even so I could see a delicate beauty underneath it all. Her hair, although a little matted and tangled, had the potential to be a sparkling chestnut mane. There was a distant look in her eyes that I'd seen a thousand times since this whole thing... the end of the world, but hers was different in a way I couldn't define or describe. We had all lost something. Some of us were more wounded by that fact than others. Some of us were even glad to have lost our old lives. Looking at this girl, this warrior, I sensed that in some ways, her life didn't begin until the world ended.

"'I'm meeting up with some friends a few clicks to the north.' She laid the sword down on the ground in front of her.

"'Bobby's in bad shape,' April said stroking his forehead. The once plump sorority girl had administered all the first aid she knew. 'We need something to clean the wound.' She brushed back her dirty blonde hair with the back of her hand. 'Plus, doesn't this mean he'll be a zombie now?'

"Tank snorted. 'You watched too many George Romero movies.'

"'Who?'

"'Romero. Night of the Living Dead. Dawn of the Dead.'

"'I thought it was Shaun of the Dead.'

"'What?' Tank growled.

"'Tank,' I said. 'Calm down.'

"'I can't take it anymore, Archie!' he shouted. 'She's wearing on my last nerve!'

"'I'm wearing on your last nerve?' she shouted back. 'You're the biggest oaf left on the planet, and I'm wearing on your last nerve?'

"'This isn't doing us any good,' I said.

"'All I said is that when people are bit by zombies they turn into zombies. Just like in that movie Shaun of the Dead.' April was screaming without restraint.

"'You ignorant little...' Tank said as he stood. 'Ahhhh, it's Dawn of the Dead. George Romero invented the friggin zombie genre...'

"Tank stopped mid dissertation when he heard a snort of laughter. His face twisted into an expression of bewilderment when he saw Lou chuckling at his expense. 'What's so funny?'

"Lou struggled to speak through the sobs of laughter. 'How are you people not dead? This has got to be the dumbest argument I have ever heard.'

"We watched her laugh for about a minute before we joined her. It was dumb. Even Bobby managed to smile.

"'Seriously,' April said as she struggled to catch her breath. 'Is Bobby going to become a zombie?'

"Lou let out one last breathy sigh of amusement and nonchalantly said, 'I don't know.'

"Our laugh fest was abruptly cut short.

"'What?' April asked.

"'Don't know,' Lou answered. 'I've never seen them leave a body behind much less leave someone alive. They usually eat everything.'

"There was a long silence after Lou spoke, too long. Her statement hung in the air like an invisible wind chime. Every once in a while, after the wind blew, you could hear the last sentence repeated. 'They usually eat everything.'

"'What are you saying?' Tank grumbled. 'Bobby could become a zombie?'

"'That's about the long and short of it,' Lou said standing. 'I guess you folks will know soon enough. He doesn't look too good.'

"She had taken three steps towards the woods before any of use moved. We were all shocked by the possibility that little Bobby could be a walking corpse at any moment.

"'Wait a minute,' I said chasing after her. 'Where you going?' "'To join my friends,' she said without slowing down.

"I turned and looked at the others. They were thinking the same thing I was. 'Can we come with you?'

"'No,' she said. No explanation. No apology. Nothing. "'Why?'

"She stopped. Back to us, her shoulders sank. She stood there. Motionless. Without turning she said, 'You'll slow me down.'

"I laughed. I'm not sure why. It was a reflex I guess. I didn't stop to analyze it at the moment. I just laughed and laughed and laughed. I couldn't stop myself.

"She finally turned. 'What's so funny?'

"'Slow you down?' I said still chuckling like a lunatic. 'Slow you down?'

"'That's what I said.'

"'Please tell me what you're late for.' I shook my head. 'Are you late for school? Work? What?' I waved her off. 'In case you haven't noticed, it ain't exactly possible to be late for anything because there ain't nothing left to be late for.'

"'My friends will start to worry,' she said sounding like her young age for the first time. 'They've been through enough.'

"'Fine,' I shouted. 'Go! We'll be fine here watching

Bobby turn into the undead.'

"April gulped. She nervously scooted away from Bobby. 'I don't want to see that,' she said.

"Lou scanned our feeble group of survivors. She looked up at the purple and black sky. I have no idea what was going through her mind. She struck me as a person who had learned to survive on instinct and her instinct was telling her to leave us behind and not give us a second thought.

"'The big one carries Bobby,' she said pointing at Tank. 'Find a weapon, and keep quiet. There's more than the skinner dead to worry about out there. We've got a lot of woods to go through before we get to a safe point. I've got bigger things to do than save you people. If we run into trouble, you fight. I don't fight for you. We clear?'

"'Why do I have to carry Bobby?' Tank protested.

"I swatted a hand in his direction signaling him to stop complaining and do as she said.

"He grunted and picked up Bobby in a fireman's carry. 'Just cause I'm big,' he said. 'It ain't fair. That's all I'm saying.'

"Tight-lipped, Lou cocked her head and gave Tank the evil eye. He quit moaning instantly. She turned, and we followed. It wouldn't be the last time she would lead us."

FOUR

"A low rumbling growl greeted us when we emerged from the woods and found ourselves on a deserted two-lane highway. The black in the sky had completely gobbled up the purple. The dimmest light broke through little vents in the thick darkness that hovered over our heads.

"The source of the growl emerged from the woods. Lumbering before us with a tremendously scarred body and face, was an enormous gorilla. It opened its mouth and flashed brilliant white canines. It rose up and pounded its chest with cupped hands, pock-pock-pock. It was a scene that would have been unheard of a few short years ago, especially on a back road in South Carolina.

"Tank, exhausted from carrying Bobby, stepped back into a pothole. The two of them went tumbling to the pavement. I raised the broken tree limb I had chosen as a weapon. It was a useless gesture with a totally useless weapon. April simply dropped to her knees and began to weep.

"Lou stepped forward and gave the beast a series of hand signals. The gorilla signaled back. A German shepherd raced out of the blackness. It was panting heavily, but didn't show any aggressiveness. In fact, it approached April and licked her tearstained face.

"The gorilla sat on its haunches and huffed. It bobbed its enormous head up and down. Lou walked over to it and put her arm around the animal's shoulder.

"''These your friends?' I asked.

"She flashed a relaxed smile that said everything. These weren't just friends. They were her home.

"The gorilla signaled to her.

"The smile disappeared. 'It was a dead end.'

"A sour grimace absorbed the gorilla's face.

"Lou stroked his back. 'We'll find him.'

"'What's this?' a voice boomed. A fat man with a bushy beard stepped onto the highway. He wore a tattered gray shirt with a name patch above the breast pocket, *Wes*.

"Lou smiled at him. 'Good to see you, too.'

"'What in tarnation do you think you're doing, Lou?' he asked, ignoring her sarcasm. 'You was supposed to follow up on Canter's lead , and find...' He shook his head. 'Instead you come back with four more...'

"'What was I supposed to do?' she asked. 'You should have seen them. I don't know how they're not already dead. No offense,' she said motioning to me.

"'None taken,' I said. 'We're not exactly sure ourselves.' "Tank stood, leaving Bobby writhing in pain on the road.

'Look here, I know a thing or two about taking care of myself, if you know what I mean.'

"'Please,' I said, 'We found you crying in a fetal position in a Wal-Mart bathroom in Athens.'

"'That's not true,' he barked. He hesitated, mulling over some fanciful lie, I'm sure, but instead cleared his throat and said, 'It was a Sam's Club.'

"'Fine! Great!' Wes threw up his arms in disgust. 'This is just great!'

"A young girl of about ten stepped out of the darkness followed by a boy of the same age. They smiled the first friendly smiles I had seen in a long, long time. They approached Bobby and knelt down beside him.

36

"'Skinner dead got a hold of this one,' the boy said pointing to Bobby's mangled shoulder.

"Wes stepped in their direction and quickly assessed Bobby's condition. 'Is that true?' he asked Lou.

"She nodded.

"'And you brought him here?'

"'I didn't,' she said. 'The big one carried him.'

"'Huh?' Tank said. 'You told me to.'

"'Is he going to become a zombie?' April asked.

"'Zombie?' Wes shook his head. 'Lord, this ain't Dawn of the Dead.'

"'Ha,' Tank screamed. 'Told you.'

"Wes shot Tank a puzzled, irritated look. 'He ain't going to turn into a zombie, but he's got a smell on him now that will attract every skinner dead within a twenty-mile radius.' He stomped the cracked highway pavement. 'Lou, you know better.'

"She shrugged her shoulders.

"'Why didn't you tell us?' I asked.

"'You would have left him,' she said.

"I would have offered an argument, but she was right. We would have left him behind or worse to save our own hides.

"'Roses,' the little girl said.

"'What are you carrying on about?' Wes asked.

"'If we pack the wound with roses, the dead won't come. They can't stand the smell of roses.'

"I was about to ask her how she knew this, but I realized it wasn't important. How does anyone know anything in this world? You learn by trial and error. And you don't want to hear the trials and errors in this place.

"'Roses?' April said. 'Where do we get roses?'

"'We passed a landscaping sign a couple miles back,' the little girl said. 'Said something about a greenhouse and orchard. We might find some there.'

"Wes breathed deeply. "'You happy?' he asked Lou. 'Now we got to backtrack cause you decided to pick up company.'

"'They're called survivors, Wes,' Lou said walking past him. 'Just like you and me.'

"He scanned our group. 'Darling, they ain't nothing like you and me.'"

***

"The greenhouse did have roses. The little girl, Valerie, trimmed the bloom off a couple of red roses and tore the petals off. She packed Bobby's wound and wrapped it with a sheet that the boy, Tyrone, had cut into bandage-sized strips. They worked together as well as any medical team I had ever seen on TV. It was obvious they had dressed wounds before. My guess was they had seen and done a lot of things kids their age should have never had to see or do. I wondered how many people they had seen die. Worse, how many had they seen killed... or killed themselves?

"We sat inside the greenhouse. It was amazing to see that the cycle of life had continued in this artificial environment without the benefit of a caretaker. Somehow the plants grew and thrived on their own. With no background in horticulture, I had no idea if that sort of thing was unusual or not. I imagined it wasn't. After all, plants grew just fine without human interference for billions of years.

"The gorilla awkwardly knuckle-walked over to our group with one arm tucked up to its chest and dumped three bottles of water at my feet. It tilted its powerful head, gave a garbled hoot-grunt and slowly sauntered away. I had no idea if gorillas could get depressed, but that ape looked

38

about as depressed as I had ever seen.

"I handed the waters to April and Tank. They were fixated on the new group of survivors, too. I sensed they were just as fascinated and frightened by them as I was. There was something different about this crew. They were more than just survivors. I could tell by their attitude, the way they communicated that they'd been through battles together. I mean battles you willingly participate in. Not like my group. We had been in battles, but only because we ran out of places to run. This new group, they looked for fights.

"I admired them, but I didn't want to have anything to do with them. They were going to die in a grand show of bravery and pride. That wasn't the way I wanted to go. In fact, I didn't want to go at all.

"As if she were reading my mind, April said, 'We aren't staying with them, are we?'

"I sipped my water and shook my head.

"'Good,' she said. 'They scare me.'

"The old man of the group, Wes, walked in from outside. He maintained an impossible paunch given the shortage of food in this world. A few dozen Twinkies wrappers on the floor of the green and yellow VW bus we traveled in to get here hinted as to his main source of food, but still, a man would have to eat an awful lot of the fat-filled treats to maintain the girth he sported.

"He approached us. 'You folks settling in all right?'

"'Fine,' I said. 'We'll be out of your hair soon.'

"He spotted a five-gallon tub of weed killer and sat his rather sizeable rear end on it. 'I want you all to know most of my goings on back there was just cause I wasn't expectin' Lou to come back with guests. It's nothing against you personally. Understand?'

"I nodded my head. 'Sure.'

"'What's your story, anyhow?'

"'What do you mean?' I asked.

"'I mean where do you come from?'

"'Come from?' I said. 'Well, last place before this was Athens...'

"'No, no,' he interrupted. 'I mean where you from? You know, your people, your kin. Me, I from a little town off I-24 in Tennessee called Manchester.'

"'Bonaroo!' April said with a shout.

"Wes smiled. 'That's right. They had that Bonaroo music festival there every year. You been?' he asked April.

"'Once,' she said nervously. 'I've never seen so many people.'

"'Me, neither,' Wes laughed. 'Lord help us, but you folks used to drive us locals crazy. You damn near doubled the population of the entire county every festival, and we didn't know what to do with you all.'

"'God, I had so much fun,' she said, and we all fell silent. Never before had something so frivolous and relatively recent seemed so meaningful and so far away.

"'I'm from Kansas City,' Tank said breaking the awkward silence. 'Lived there my whole life.'

"'The Chiefs,' Wes responded.

"Tank smiled. 'Don't get me started.'

"'Please, you're talking to a Titans fan. We were a foot away from winning the Super Bowl.'

"I looked around, and they all had smiles. I didn't know why, but it made me angry. How could they smile and reminisce in the face of where we were and what we had been through?

"'You?' Wes asked. 'What about you?'

"'What about me?'

"'Who was your team?'

"'My team?' I said.

"'Yeah, who did you pull for?'

"I looked him in the eyes and said, 'I can't see how that could possibly matter.' There was an audible gasp from April, and Tank looked at me slack jawed.

"Wes squinted his left eye and thought of a thousand different ways he could rearrange the nose on my face, but he didn't act on his anger. Instead, he breathed deeply and stood up. 'You folks are welcome to tag along as long as you want.' He gave me an accommodating nod and walked back outside.

"April and Tank didn't speak.

"'Ignorant red neck,' I said.

"'I don't know,' April said. 'Seemed nice enough.'

"'Ahhh,' I said waving her off. I stood and exited the greenhouse. I was beginning to feel trapped by the small space and the conversation was irritating the hell out of me.

"I couldn't believe the fat-ass had asked me what my story was. My story was my family was gone. Why the hell would I want to chitchat about something like that? I was married. So what? Got married right out of high school. Had a kid, a boy. So what? It didn't matter anymore. They were gone. Lost them to this punk-crap world, if you must know.

"I quickly walked away from the others. I knew what was coming. I got like this every once in awhile. When I would remember. Think about them. I would cry like a baby. The others didn't need to see how much I missed them. They didn't need to know that it felt like my heart was being pricked with pins whenever I faced the fact that they were gone. Dead, at least I hoped they were. I wished them dead. I didn't want them to be one of those purple jerks, or the skinner dead, or any of the other monster-freaks that had taken over the world. I didn't want that for them.

"That was the hell of it. I was a husband and a father whose only real hope was that his wife and kid were dead. That's the kind of world I was left with.

"I found a stump on the edge of the orchard and sat down. A legion of withered trees stretched out before me. It was acres of evidence of the fragile and feeble nature of our old world. Skeletons of trees that once bore blossoms and fruit and fluttering leaves were now dry, hulking, twisted pieces of wood that were just waiting to fall. I realized sitting there that I was one of them. I was waiting to fall, too.

"I rubbed my hands together and fought not to cry. I tried to tell myself that it served no purpose. I wouldn't feel better afterward. I wouldn't get a great sense of relief out of it. My family would still be gone, but my throat would hurt and my eyes would burn. But I couldn't talk myself out of it. The tears came. The snot dripped. And the hurt engulfed me. I sniffed and snorted. I asked the alien sky why, but got no answer. My story. This was my story. Is this what Wes wanted to know, that I was a coward for letting my family die?

"I stopped mid-sob when I heard a rustling in the trees to my right. A shadow of a figure approached. An animal. A gorilla. It plodded towards me. Its sad eyes fixated on me from under its scarred brow. It stopped at my feet and sat down. It sighed deeply and turned and looked out to the orchard. It had lost something, too. It had come here for the same reason I had. It dropped its powerful head and picked at the infertile ground in front of it. I reached out slowly and patted its shoulder. I chuckled at the absurdity of it, me crying at the edge of a dead orchard patting the shoulder of the saddest gorilla on the planet. This was the world I lived in, the world without my wife and son."

FIVE

"I slept at the foot of the tree stump next to the dead orchard. My choice for a place to sleep is not as unusual as the fact that I slept at all. Sleep is a rare commodity when you are prey. That's what we humans were now, prey. We were other creatures' food and slave labor. They even hunted us for sport.

"Most of the reason I was able to nod off is because of the 400-pound gorilla named Ajax that decided to sleep next to me. The gentle sound of his breathing lulled me to a point where I couldn't help but nod off. I felt... at ease. A feeling I didn't think was possible in this world.

"If I slept at ease that is not how I woke up. I awoke to Ajax's panicked growling. Startled, I popped up from my slumped over position and wiped the drool from my chin. The dog, Kimball, barked frantically toward the orchard. What passed for a day in this world had broken. Everything was cast in violet hue. I scrambled to my feet facing the direction the two animals faced. I saw nothing, but heard a low, steady chatter in my head that grew in intensity with every passing minute. I backed away, stumbling over exposed roots, but never falling.

"'What?' I asked Ajax and Kimball. They, of course, did not answer. They simply continued their hysterics. Ajax pounded his chest, pock-pock-pock, pock-pock-pock.

"I saw the branches of the dead trees in the back of the orchard move. An animal, scratch that, a herd of animals was slowly heading towards us. An animal I had never seen before. The chatter intensified. I covered my ears, but the noise was inside my head.

"'Silencers,' I barely heard a voice say. I turned to see Lou standing at the ready with her sword.

"'What?'

"'Silencers,' she repeated. 'Nothing to worry about. They're working with us.'

"I shook my head. 'You mean you. I'm not working with anybody.'

"She shrugged her shoulders. 'If that's the way you want it.'

"'I do,' I said. Ajax was growing more and more agitated. He huffed and gritted his massive teeth. 'Your gorilla doesn't seem too thrilled,' I said.

"'I don't blame him,' she said. 'They cut out his tongue.'

"She said it with such a nonchalant tone that I couldn't believe she'd actually said it. I must have heard her wrong. I had to have. 'His tongue?'

"She nodded. 'They didn't eat it though.'

"She said this as if it was a great gesture of goodwill by the Silencers.

"'That's great...' I stopped mid-thought. I got my first glimpse of a Silencer. It had a human torso and head, only the head was upside down. The mouth (where the forehead should be) appeared to be sewn shut in a dreadful frown. The bottom half of the creature was a four-legged crab. It bore a single spike at the end of each leg and five deadly spikes at the end of each hand.

"'A new one,' I heard in my head.

"I breathed in and almost choked.

"'Relax,' Lou said. 'I told you they're working with us.'

"'A fresh, delicious tongue,' a raspy voice said in my

head. 'I just need a little taste.'

"'Do they know that?' I said to Lou, backing away.

"'Most of them,' she smiled.

"If she was joking, I didn't get it.

"She rolled her eyes. 'You see that one?' She pointed to a Silencer in the middle of the orchard. He looked no different from the others except for a chain with a tongue hanging around his neck.

"'Ye-Yeah,' I said.

"'That's Canter. He's the leader. He's the only one that matters. The rest of them do what he says.'

"The group of about twenty Silencers reached us. They swayed and sniffed the air. One broke from the pack and stepped forward. Ajax roared and leapt toward it. Another Silencer advanced. Ajax pounded the ground, and Kimball's hackles were up. He barked incessantly.

"'Wow,' I said. 'Y'all work really well together.'

"'Ajax! Kimball!' Lou screamed. 'Back!'

"Wes and the others (including my crew) approached from behind us.

"The one Lou called Canter looked me up and down.

"'Picked them up last night. Following your dead-end lead,' she said with no attempt to hide the irritation in her voice. "Canter glared at her.

"'Every lead you've given me has been a dead-end. I'm starting to think you don't want me to find him.'

"Canter moved forward.

"'It's getting harder and harder to believe you.'

"It was obvious they were having a conversation, but I couldn't hear Canter's half. I turned to others to see if they could hear the ugly crab-thingy.

"'None of that,' Wes said. 'Damn it now. Pipe us all in or don't talk at all.'

"Canter and Wes exchanged a stern look. The ugly

creature then focused on Lou.

"'Do it,' she said. There was a pause. 'Just do it!'

"'Do not take that tone with me,' a voice said in my head. 'This alliance is held together with the thinnest of threads. You would be advised not to push me too far.'

"Lou took a deep breath. 'I... I'm sorry. It's just that we need all ears on this. It's too important.'

"Canter stepped forward, eyes still zeroed in on Lou. 'Very well. Keep in mind, General Roy and his swarm are still officially ruling this world. I can't guarantee they can't pick up on this transmission.'

"'I haven't seen a Délon in two weeks,' Wes said. 'Word is they've lost control of the north and most of the west.'

"'Wrong,' Canter replied sharply. 'Not lost. Losing. General Roy's never been more dangerous.'

"Kimball sniffed the ground and approached the group of Silencers to the right of Canter. They nervously scampered from him. They looked like a group of fiddler crabs darting across the beach.

"'You're running out of time,' Canter said. 'They've captured two more Storytellers. And they hold two Keepers.'

"I turned to Tank and April to see if they understood the nonsense we were hearing. They both shrugged and then their eyes widened as if they were suddenly terrified. I turned back to find Canter's upside down face just inches from mine.

"'The new one is a liability,' he said fixated on my mouth. "'I-I-I,' is all I managed to say.

"'It's none of your concern,' Lou said.

"Canter shifted his attention to her. 'Everything you do is my concern. You don't seem to appreciate what I'm risking.'

"She laughed.

"'You dare laugh at me,' he barked advancing on her. Ajax grunted and stepped in front of her.

"Canter faltered. He examined the ape's face and then chuckled hideously. He held out the tongue hanging around his neck. 'Missing something?'

"Ajax roared and leapt forward. Kimball turned and bounded toward them. All hell was about to break loose.

"'Enough!' Lou screamed. Ajax and Kimball instantly heeded her command. 'We don't have time for this!'

"Canter chuckled again. 'Take your orders, ape.'

"'Back off, Canter. Don't think we don't know why you're helping us. If the Délons fall, you're in control. So, don't tell me about the risks you're taking. Just tell me where to find him!'

"'Him who?' I asked without thinking. It was none of my business, and I didn't want to make it my business.

"Canter turned to me. 'Curious boy.'

"I swallowed and shook my head. 'Not really.'

"'Then hold your tongue. Your sweet, delicious tongue!'

"I could hear the other Silencers smack their sewn lips. I grit my teeth and fought back the bile.

"'I told you before,' Lou said. 'He's none of your concern. Now, I assume you're here because you have new information.'

"He slowly turned from me to her. 'The Bashir are advancing from the west.'

"'What's the Bashir?' she asked.

"'Ask your new friend,' Canter said.

"'New friend?' Wes said.

"Lou shot me a sideways glance.

"'Me,' I said. I turned to April and Tank. 'Or us, rather. He's talking about us.'

"'Okay then, what's the Bashir?' Lou asked me. The trust had vanished from her tone.

"'Ugly cusses,' Tank said. All eyes shifted to him. 'Hard to describe, really. Massive heads. Tusks that curve back, nearly touch their giant slimy eyeballs. Thick hands the size of Texas watermelons...'

"'They stink to high heaven,' April added.

"'Yeah,' Tank concurred. 'Big, mean, and smelly. That about sums it up. Seen one squash a guy like a bug near Memphis. Guts and mess all over the place...'

"'We get the point,' Lou said, her gaze still fixed on me. "'That's a Bashir,' I said timidly. 'But I don't see what that has to do with me.'

"Canter leaned in and sniffed me. He was so close he raised goose bumps on my flesh. 'I know your smell, creyshaw.' "'Creyshaw?' I said backing away. 'What's a creyshaw?' "He laughed. 'You are a creyshaw.'

"Back-off, Canter," Lou said.

"Canter complied and moved to the edge of the orchard. 'The Bashir are hunting your creyshaw,' he said. 'I told you, he is trouble.'

"'What's a creyshaw?' I demanded.

"'We can handle the Bashir,' Wes said.

"Canter shook his head. 'Even the Délons fear the Bashir. They are one of the reasons the Délons are so desperate to find the Source.'

"'What's a creyshaw?' No one was listening to me.

"'What about, Oz?' Lou asked, her voice shrill and panicked. She was on the verge of losing her cool.

"Canter took a step in between the first row of trees in the orchard and turned back. 'They keep him on the move and away from the collective. The swarm does not know where he is. Only General Roy and a few others know. I have agents close to the general. We will know soon enough.'

"'You said it yourself, we don't have much time,' she said.

"'You don't,' Canter said walking away. 'But if you fail, I will merely find another way to get what I want.'

"'Canter!' Lou screamed.

"'Travel east,' he said. 'General Roy is headed toward the coast. I will gather what information I can. Don't be surprised if next time we meet, I have news of your Oz's demise.'

"'You bring me back that news,' Lou said in a hushed tone. 'I'll kill you.'

"Canter and the other Silencers laughed.

"In a state of shock, I watched Lou and Ajax walk away. I caught a glimpse of Wes's anguished face as he turned and headed back to the greenhouse. Tank looked at me and shook his head while April smiled timidly.

"Valerie whistled, and Kimball bolted towards her. Tyrone looked at me with sympathetic eyes.

"'Anybody going to tell me what a creyshaw is?' I asked."

***

"'A creyshaw is a coward,' Tyrone said.

"'Or a warrior,' Valerie added.

"Tyrone rolled his eyes and nodded, reluctantly agreeing with her. 'Yeah, yeah, sure, but that never has made sense to me.'

"April, Tank, Valerie, Tyrone, and I all sat around a small open pit fire. We were feasting on a meal of canned pears.

"'Has to mean one or the other,' Tank said with a mouth full of pear.

"'Maybe,' Valerie answered. 'Have to ask the Silencers. It's their word.'

"April shivered at the thought. 'I'd just as soon never see them again. What were those things?'

"'I don't know,' Tyrone said digging a juicy pear chunk out of his can with a fork. 'One of the Storytellers thought it up.' "'What is this Storyteller business?' I asked.

"Valerie looked at me surprised. 'You don't know?' "I shook my head. 'Should I?'

"'It's why we're here,' Tyrone said. 'Dealing with the monsters and the undead and whatever else is out there. Ain't you wondered how we all got here?'

"Tank looked at Tyrone cockeyed. 'Wondered? That's all I pretty much do from the time I wake up 'til I go to sleep. Only a crazy man don't wonder.'

"Tyrone smiled. 'Wonder no more, my friend. For I have all the answers... Well I have most of them.'

"Valerie shook her head in disapproval.

"'All right, all right,' Tyrone said. 'I have some answers. Does that work?' he asked Valerie.

"She smiled. 'Better.'

"He stuck his tongue out at her in a show of mock annoyance. Back to me, 'Check it out,' he said. 'There's these Storytellers, they were this bunch of retards...'

"'Tyrone,' Valerie protested.

"'Sorry, sorry, I mean mentally challenged kids that went to this shrink guy. He taught them...' He thought about where to go from here. 'I'm not exactly sure what he taught them. It's like magic, I guess.' He turned to Valerie. 'What do they call that again?'

"'HMI,' she said. 'Hyper Mental Imaging, and it's not magic. It's science. He taught them a way to visualize and help them cope with their disability.'

"'Right,' Tyrone nodded. 'What she said. This shrink

51

taught them to visualize stuff, like having a good day, or that they were smarter than they really were, you know. It worked pretty good. Too good. They began visualizing things, and it would happen. You get it?'

"I turned to Tank and April hoping they would chime in, but they didn't. I shook my head.

"'Stuff that was happening in their minds started happening in the real world.'

"Tank shook his head. 'You're crazy.'

"'What's so crazy about that?' Tyrone asked.

"'You're saying a bunch of retarded kids dreamed up all these monsters, and that's that?' Tank said sounding incredulous. "'You got a better explanation?' Tyrone asked.

"'Where do you think these monsters came from?' Valerie asked.

"Tank scanned our faces. Nothing he could come up with sounded as plausible as Tyrone's explanation. He shrugged his shoulders. 'Nuclear fallout.'

"'Nuclear what?' Tyrone asked.

"'You know,' Tank grunted. 'Fallout from a nuclear bomb.'

"'Nuclear bomb,' Valerie snickered. 'What nuclear bomb?'

"Tank tossed his empty can of pears to the ground. 'Just because we didn't see a nuclear bomb doesn't mean one didn't go off or three or four or a thousand. They could have gone off on the other side of the planet for all we know. The nuclear fallout, radiation poisoning, whatever you want to call it, still could impact us. Ain't that right, Archie?'

"'It wasn't a nuclear bomb,' I said.

"'Tank laughed. 'You believe this crap?'

"'It ain't about believing,' Tyrone said. 'The Storytellers are real. We saved one of them. Got him to his Keeper.

Right?' he asked Valerie.

"'Right,' she answered. 'Fought the Takers. Kicked their asses.'

"'Whoa!' Tyrone screamed as he gave Valerie a high five.

"'Language,' a voice said from outside the circle. Lou stepped forward, sword at her hip, hair hidden beneath a red bandana. 'Your momma may not be around to kick your butt for cussing, Val, but I am. You understand me?'

"Valerie nodded sheepishly.

"'We're just filling the newbies in on the Storyteller business,' Tyrone said.

"'Yeah, well wrap it up. We've got to get moving?' She turned to me. 'Your group joining us, creyshaw?'

"I narrowed my eyes and shot her a disapproving look. 'We'll be fine on our own.'

"She chuckled. 'I doubt that.' She turned to leave and then stopped. 'Your friend Little Bobby has been asking for you in the greenhouse. If he's too much for you guys to handle, we'll take him with us.'

"Part of me wanted them to take him. I seriously doubted our group's ability to take care of him and survive. I felt like with us it was an either-or proposition. Lou's attitude was beginning to grate on me so I said, 'We can take care of our own.'

"She chuckled again. 'That's not what you were saying last night.'

"I stood. 'Things change.'

"She gave me a lingering stare. I could sense she was trying to see what was different. Without another word, she walked off. "Tyrone chased after her.

"Valerie picked up the discarded pear cans. Before leaving she asked, 'You decide which one you are yet?'

"'What do you mean?' I asked.

"'Which kind of creyshaw, the warrior or the coward?'

"I looked at Tank and April for support, but they both looked away. Valerie waited patiently, almost pleasantly, for an answer. I walked away without giving her one."

***

"I entered the greenhouse and marveled at what was not apparent to me in the dim, almost absent light of the previous night. Not only had the plants inside this glass enclosure survived, they had flourished. Every plant's leaves were an almost impossible green. The blooms were a variety of rich, vibrant colors. The world outside this building was a dead, corrosive terrain, but in here, it was a Garden of Eden.

"April and Tank were awestruck too by the daylight viewing of the greenhouse. I don't think any of us ever expected to see something this... alive again.

"Little Bobby was propped up against a stack of fifty-pound fertilizers bags. He flashed us a goofy grin as we approached. 'Hey,' he said. His voice as high-pitched and squeaky as ever. 'I thought you left me.'

"'Couldn't leave Little Bobby behind, now could we?' I said. "'Not a chance,' Tank added.

"April squatted and placed a warm hand on his leg. 'How are you feeling?'

"'Better,' Little Bobby squawked. 'You know what I was thinking?'

"'What?' she asked.

"'I was thinking I wish I could ride a horse again.'

"She patted his leg. 'Someday, Bobby. Someday.'

"'I miss the horses,' he said.

"Little Bobby was a simple man. He had the mind of a child at times. He could ride a horse like he was born for it, but he really wasn't much good for anything else. He tried to stand again, but could only manage to lift himself off the floor a few inches before he flopped back down.

"'Tired, boss man,' he said looking at me. 'We gotta go now?'

"I shook my head. 'What are we in a hurry for?'

"'Huh?' he asked, missing my sarcastic tone.

"'Rest,' I said. 'We've got time.'

"April plopped down on the floor next to him and leaned back against the fertilizer bags. Little Bobby leaned his head on her shoulder.

"Tank and I exited the greenhouse. Tank took a tentative look back at the glass enclosure. 'Little Bobby kind of got shorted in the brain department, didn't he?'

"I nodded. 'Suppose, but then again none of use are genius material."

"'Seriously, he's really dumb,' Tank said without an ounce of remorse or cruelty. 'I mean he's a dumby's dumby.'

"I smiled despite all efforts not to. 'That's enough.'

"'You know,' Tank continued, 'I once asked him if he knew what two plus two was. You know what he said?'

"'What?' I asked.

"'Penguin,' Tank replied.

"I tried to hold it in, but laughter gushed from my mouth.

"'I'm serious,' Tank said.

"I slapped my thigh and continued to howl.

"'I'm not joking,' Tank pleaded. 'What?' He watched me in disbelief for a few seconds more and then he joined in on the laughter.

"'That can't be true,' I said as I heaved.

"'I swear,' Tank said sighing deeply. "Hand to God." He held up his right hand.

"'Okay, so he's not that smart. You're not that good looking, and I'm not that tall. We've all got our problems.'

"I stopped laughing as I saw Lou and the others pack up the van. Part of me felt the need to go with them. They were much more adept at this survival stuff than my crew and me. Truth be known, the fact that we were still alive was pure luck.

"'Lou loaded Kimball into the van and then turned to me. 'Last chance,' she said. 'We could use you.'

"Without sounding the least bit convincing I said, 'We'll be fine.'

"'I'm sure you will,' she said sounding even less convincing.

"Ajax stuck his head out of the van's side door and grunted. He gestured with his hand and dipped back inside the van. Lou shook her head.

"'What?' I asked. 'Did he say something?'

"'Yeah," she answered. 'He did.' She shut the van door.

"'What did he say?'

"'He said your hour is up.'

"'Wait... What?'"

Oz

SIX

"I have another patient coming in," Dr Graham says. "Your hour is up."

I hear Scoop-face clear his throat and stir. "What?"

"Wide awake, now. C'mon, we don't have much time."

"Doc... I wasn't finished."

"You are for today."

I hear the sound of a chair scraping across a wood floor. The door to Dr. Graham's office opens.

"He giving you any trouble, Dr. Graham?" Chester asks.

"Not at all. We're just a little lethargic from the regression."

"Doc," Scoop-face grunts. "I have so much more to say... I was just getting to the good part."

"We'll take it up next time," Dr. Graham says with just a hint of impatience.

"Tomorrow?" Scoop-face asks.

"Tomorrow? You're not on the schedule until..." There is a pause as I imagine Dr. Graham is looking through an appointment book or PDA or blackberry, whatever is used in this time. "Looks like three days from now."

"Tomorrow, Doc. C'mon do an old, faceless jackass a favor. I ain't never asked for anything before."

Another pause. This time he is contemplating Scoop-face's request. "Very well. Tomorrow, noon. I have a couple of hours open."

"You're a saint, Doc," Scoop-face says. "A saint."

"C'mon, Archie," Chester says. "Let's go."

The door closes.

***

I wander the yellow-lined halls after I leave the janitor's closet. Bones is close in tow. He talks of snarkle, hambone, and the others as we walk. Even if they are just a nonsensical string of words they seem to soothe his shattered psyche, and truth-be-known, I feel better the more he brings them up. So, I let him talk with very little input from me.

I turn Scoop-face's session over and over again in my mind. I picture Lou coming to his rescue in the woods, Wes chowing down on snack cakes, Kimball wagging his tail, Valerie and Tyrone finding a moment to play and joke despite the fact the world was falling apart around them, and Ajax - I could see his sad and noble face staring back at me in my mind's eye. His steely stare is telling me something. He is disappointed in me. I've let him down. More than that. I...

"Boss," Bones barks.

I turn to him.

"You all right?"

"What?"

His right eye twitches. "You went away... I mean you were gone, man." He whistles. "La-la land, my friend."

"I'm fine." I try to capture the image of Ajax in my mind again, but he's gone. "Just visiting old friends," I say with a smile.

"Yeah," Bones says. "Happens a lot around here."

"How long you say you been here?" I ask.

He chuckles. "That's the million dollar question, boss.

Nobody knows how long they been here. That's why they make places like this."

I look at him with a narrowed glare. "Explain."

"Time, the way we think things work... alarm clocks, lollipops, baseball, checkers... all those things that used to be... you know, our lives. They want us to think it's still out there, but it isn't."

"It isn't?"

"Oh, no, man. That stuff is gone. Way gone. There is nothing out there. There's not even an out there out there. You get it?"

I stare and consider his statement. "No," I answer. "Not at all."

"Think about it, boss. Have you seen an exit sign in this place?"

I think about it. He doesn't give me time to answer.

"Of course you haven't," he shrieks. "Because there is no place to exit to. It's all in here." He pats the wall to his right. "There is no out there out there. Get it? It's all in here." This time he points to his head. "In here." He pokes me in the forehead.

"Damn," a voice booms from the other end of the hall. Chester approaches. "The man's first day with a GP pass since he's been here and you're trying to fill his head with crazy talk. He's got enough insane snaking around in that head of his. He don't need yours in there, too."

Bones's eyes nearly jump out of his head at the sound of Chester's voice. He whispers to me, "Remember who helped you today, boss. I did."

I nod.

"That means I get to go back with you."

Still approaching, Chester shouts. "Break it up, you two. Get back to your rooms."

"Back?" I say to Bones, but Chester thinks I'm talking

to him.

"Yeah, back as in return to your rooms now!"

"On it, Mr. Chester," Bones says, all the while still looking at me. "Back is the only way to go."

"Back," I say.

Bones turns and walks with almost a skip in his step. "Back is the only way out of here, ain't that right, boss man?" The question is directed to Chester, but I know he's talking to me.

"Ain't no way out of here, thin man," Chester says as he passes Bones. He stops a few feet from me. "Back, up, down, east, west, anyway you go all leads to one place, you understand me?" Chester asks.

I don't answer.

"Here," he says. "There is no other place in your life except here. You ain't near as crazy as the others in this place. You want to hold on to what you have left of your mind you remember that one thing. Here is all there is." He steps past me. "Your room, now."

***

As I drift off to a restless sleep, the dead gather at the foot of my bed. Their eyes are inert and penetrating at the same time. A woman, her head flopping on a broken neck, reaches for me and touches my foot over the blanket. I jerk my foot back, but it is a reflex. I am not afraid of her. I don't know if it's because they've visited so many times that I've grown used to them, or if it's because they look different. They no longer look angry to me. They look sad. They look like they need my help.

I throw back the covers and stand. The dead follow my every move. I take a step toward them. A hand reaches out from under the bed and grabs my ankle. I am back to being scared. I jump back and shuffle across the room, ramming into the door. A loud click echoes through the room and the door opens. The dead smile.

I wait for someone to enter, Nurse Kline or Chester. They surely were close by. The door does not just open on its own. They are monitoring my every move. But seconds turn into minutes, and no one comes. The dead are inching their way closer to me. They want me to leave. I don't want to. If I'm caught out in the hall, I will be... I don't know what will happen to me, but I can't imagine it will be good.

The dead creature that had grabbed my ankle begins to crawl out from under my bed. He or she or it is not like the others. It is big and... not human. It's a huge hulking beast that is covered in hair and slime. It's a Taker, and the anger that was absent in the other dead is frighteningly apparent in his tooth-filled snarl.

Suddenly, being caught in the hallway is the least of my worries. I pull the door open and run out into the corridor. The brightness of the flickering fluorescent lights nearly blinds me. I squint against the glare and wait for someone to come running, to be busted for escaping my prison, but no one comes. I am alone in the hallway.

I look back at my room. The Taker snaps its jaws in the doorway. Going back is not an option. I run fully expecting to be stopped by someone on the hospital staff at any moment.

I do not pay attention to the corridors I turn down. I just run. When I started, I was following the yellow line, but the line beneath my feet is now blue. I am not authorized to mingle with the blue line people. I am in real trouble now.

I run until I can't catch my breath. I stop and pant and grunt and wallow in general misery. I don't know how far

I've gone. A sharp pain throbs from underneath my rib cage. My throat is dry. I hear a crash from behind me and decide to walk quickly to the next series of hallways just ahead.

The lines end here. No blue, no yellow, no red or green. Nothing. I have an option to go left or right, but both hallways are dark, almost black. Another crash from behind me convinces me going back is not a viable choice, and a scream from the hallway to my left makes my decision somewhat easier. The pitch-black hallway to my right is the least of the three evils. I slowly make my way down the hall.

A whisper floats through the dark air, "Oz."

I exhale through pursed lips. I am walking into something, an ambush, a slaughter, an end to my rather confused existence.

"Oz," the whispering voice repeats. But I realize its not traveling through the air. It is in my head. I hear a series of heavy clicks. They come from all around me.

All light is gone now. I cannot see anything, but I can feel movement all around me. I stop. It's pointless to go on. Something brushes against my leg and I can feel movement beneath my bare feet. I reach for the wall to my right, but it's not there. I reach to my left and feel a cold, damp raised surface. It is a rock.

I hear more clicking and what sounds like water dripping. The stuffy air of the hospital is gone. The air is cool and damp. A sliver of light appears above me, ten feet or so. My immediate surroundings become illuminated. I am in a hole... no, it's a small cave. I can see the rock wall to my left, but the right wall is out of sight. A small creek clicks and gurgles and burps on the cave floor to my right. It disappears underneath a wall of rocks in front of me.

There are a series of footholds leading up to the sliver

of light. I climb and only then spot the source of movement beneath my feet. The cave floor is covered in millions of bugs, some of which are still clinging to my feet. I frantically shake them off and climb as fast I can.

The sliver of light is a tiny crawl space. I cannot tell how long it is, and there is just barely enough room for me to fit. I look back and see that the bugs are now making their way up the cave wall. I push my way through the opening and hoped the crawl space either gets bigger or leads to an opening I can fit through, because it is apparent I could not go back.

I crawl on my belly, pushing myself forward with my elbows. I can hear the bugs entering the opening of the crawl space. Their tiny legs make horrendous scrapping noise as they make their way toward me. I crawl faster, my back now touching the top of the crawl space. It isn't getting wider. It is narrowing, and the source of the light is no closer.

I flatten myself as much as I can. No longer pushing myself forward with my elbows, my arms are extended forward, and I'm pulling myself with my finger tips. My butt is wedged. I can no longer pull myself forward. I feel the bugs probing my feet. A slight stinging around my ankles as I imagine some have begun to bite.

I feel something grab my wrists. I am dragged forward. This is not a bug… I hope. Because if it is, it is enormous. I look and see... mud covered hands pulling me through the opening. I am pulled with such force, the crawl space is expanding all around me. That's when I realize the space is made up of a sludge like clay.

I burst through the opening and fall to the creek on the cave floor. I have made it through to the other side. I sit up on my hands and knees. I am covered in mud. I turn to watch the bugs flow through the opening like water coming out of a faucet, but they never appear.

I stand, anxious and breathing irregularly. I am in an enormous chamber made of clay walls that are some forty feet high. Bright fires are peppered throughout the cavern making the temperature considerably hotter than on the other side of the crawl space. I estimate the square footage of this place to be about 1,500 to 2,000 feet. It is the closest thing to a naturally formed grand ballroom that I have ever seen.

A silhouette of a man stands in front of the nearest fire. He is scrawny and crooked. His posture suggests a feeble old man, but given the strength of this grip I know that appearances can be deceiving.

"Who are you?" I ask.

He does not answer. His white eyes shine through the darkness. Strands of long, thick hair hang from his head.

"You arranged for this... You wanted me to come here." I say. A snicker is followed by a grotesque hacking.

I move to the right trying to get a look at his face. I see purple faces peering out of the darkest corner of the cavern. Startled, I fixate on them.

"You are the key," the old man says.

My attention back to him. "The key to what?"

More hacking. "Must you ask the same questions every time?"

Confused I say, "We've done this before?"

"A thousand times. More."

A slash of light reveals a portion of his face. It is... purple. His eyes are milky white. He is Délon. I ready myself for an attack.

"You are the key to the Source! I must have the Source!" It steps into the full light. His body is as feeble as his silhouette hinted. His face is cracked and wrinkled.

When he talks, I can hear his blackened tongue rubbing against his mandibles.

"The Source?"

"Yes. The Source!" He groans. "I cannot take this endless loop. The Source. Bring me the Source."

"I don't..."

"You don't know what it is. I know that. You've told me more times than I can count."

"Why would I help you?"

He pounds the clay wall next to him. He is on the verge of a fit, but restrains himself. He points to the corner of the cavern where the purple faces are peering out at me. "I'm too tired to escort you over there. See for yourself."

I hesitate. I take a step in that direction and then pause. I wipe my muddy hand across my face. I resume my journey to the darkened corner. As I get closer, I discover the purple faces are attached to disembodied heads crammed into the clay walls of the cavern. I am so mesmerized by them that I don't see the body on the gurney until I nearly run into it.

I look at it closely. The face is hidden beneath a shunter. It is a young boy, fifteen... sixteen. It's me. A young curly headed boy of the same age, so caked with mud that he blends in with the cave wall, steps out of the black corner. Gordy.

"I'm watching him for you," he says.

"You're real," I say not knowing if it's true.

He looks at me strangely. "Well, duh."

"I don't understand. Why am I here?"

"To help us decorate the place, why do you think, you moron. C'mon, we can't keep doing this." He directs his attention to the old Délon. "Can't you give him some kind of memory jolt or zap or whatever? We go through this every time."

"I'm not a magician!" The Délon shouts.

Back to me. "Listen," Gordy says. "The purple pile of puss needs the Source to get his power back. You are the key to the Source. He knows it. I know it. General Roy knows it. Every Destroyer on the planet knows it."

"Destroyer?"

"Monsters, freaks... the things the Storytellers created to get back at the world for treating them like a pile of dog crap. Understand?"

I look at myself lying on the gurney. I shake my head.

"It's not important." He puts his hand on my shoulder. "Focus. The Source. You have to find it. The Délons have got you trapped in here." He taps the shunter, and it squeals. "This little guy is drilling out your brain and replacing it with purple mush. Everything you think is real ain't real. You got to find a way out and get back to finding the Source, and you got to do it soon because I am bored out of my ever-lovin' mind down here."

I turn and watch as the old Délon begins to wheeze and cough. "Why is he helping us?" I ask.

Gordy stifles a frustrated scream. "Oz Griffin meet the Pure. Pure meet Oz Griffin."

"The Pure?" I say. I examine his twisted body. "Canter wasn't lying."

"He was," the Pure croaks. "He always lies."

"He said you were alive."

"He had no idea it was true. No one knows I'm alive."

"What am I?" Gordy snaps. "Chopped liver?"

"Pardon," The Pure moans. "No one of real consequence knows."

"Nice," Gordy says shaking his head. "After all I've done for you, and this is the thanks I get? Insults? You ugly bag of bones."

With that, the Pure leaps across the cavern and lands

on Gordy forcing him to the ground. "I should tear open your skull and dine on your useless gray matter." The Pure is indeed not as feeble as he looks.

Gordy screams.

I push the Pure off of him. The old Délon snaps his mandibles in anger and frustration.

"What is our deal?" I ask the Pure.

He looks at me. He is breathing heavily and staggering. The leap across the room drained what little energy he had. "Your world for the Source."

"My world?"

Gordy stands. "Home, Oz. Home."

"You mean..."

"Everything as you remember it. As I've told you a thousand times before. Your world."

My mind tries to grab hold of the concept, but I can't. A lump forms in my throat, and I fight back a tear. "I don't remember."

"You do," Gordy says. "Or you can again."

"How?"

He walks over to the nearest clay wall and writes with his finger - *Millie B. Story.*

I read the name over and over again.

"Who..."

"Shhhhh," he says. "The next session is about to start."

The light slowly begins to lose way to the darkness. Within a matter of seconds, it is pitch black. I soon hear muffled voices from overhead. I stand on my toes to see if I can hear the voices more clearly.

My eyes begin to acclimate to the darkness. Slowly, I can make out shapes. A mop handle, a shelf with cleaning supplies. I am back in the janitor's closet.

"Getting sleepy, now," Dr. Graham's voice traveling down from the vent. "Almost there. You're feeling relaxed and safe. Safe, Archie. We are back in the woods with your friends."

Scoop‾face

SEVEN

"We didn't fair too well without Lou and the others. Barely a week had passed when April squatted in a patch of poison ivy. She was covered in red welts.

"Tank caught a nasty cold shortly after that. He was snorting, sniffing and basically leaking mucus from every hole in his head.

"We found a box of fruit cocktail behind an abandoned backwoods convenience store. The cans were rusted and beat up, but I was hungry so I took a chance none of the others would. I threw up for three days.

"Little Bobby was the only one who seemed to be doing better. His bite was on the mend , and he was in general good spirits. For most of the waking day, he sang the only song he knew, 'I've Got Friends In Low Places.' And by the second hour of the first day he took to singing, the rest of us hoped to the heavens above that Garth Brooks had survived the end of the world so we could find him and give him the beating of a lifetime for writing that damn song.

"His choice of song did lead to an interesting conversation though. April began to wonder out loud where all the famous people were. The ones she used to read about in supermarket tabloids and on the Internet.

"'Like Paris Hilton,' she said as she scratched her forearm raw. 'You reckon she survived.'

"'Lord, I hope not,' Tank said with a nasally tone. 'That girl wasted all her pretty in normal times. I can't imagine God would give her a second chance.'

"I laughed. 'What makes you so sure God's got a hand in what happened here?'

"Tank gave me a perplexed look. 'God's got a hand in everything.'

"'Those crab things we saw,' I said. 'And the purple... people and the Bashir.... You think God's got a hand in that, too?'

"Tank spat a big gob of snot on a nearby tree. 'I ain't a preacher. Don't know nothing about the Bible. I just know what my momma taught me. God is everywhere and has a hand in everything.'

"'What about Angelina?' April said ignoring our religious discussion. 'You think she made it?'

"Tank's eyes lit up. 'Now, that I wouldn't mind. She was pretty and smart and did stuff for poor people... or something to that effect.'

"'Oh, and Brad, too,' April said excitedly. 'I bet he made it.' "'Ahh, don't nobody need him around,' Tank moaned. 'I'd like a crack at that Angelina without him interfering.'

"April howled with laughter. 'Angelina wouldn't have you if you were the last man on earth.'

"'Hell,' Tank said. 'I ain't far off.'

"'What about Archie,' April said. 'He might like to hook up with her.'

"I shook my head. 'Nah, Tank can have her.' The truth was I was still in love with my wife. The end of the world didn't change that. Tank was welcome to all the Hollywood starlets and models and beauty queens we came across. My heart belonged to the one and only woman I ever loved.

"'I hope Homer Simpson is still alive,' Little Bobby said. 'He was funny.'

"We all stopped to look at him.

"'What?' he asked.

"Tank was about to say something, but I stopped him. 'Nothing, Bobby.'

"Tank, April, and I began to laugh as we resumed our travels.

"That's how we traveled most of the time. We talked about nothing important and stopped to laugh at little Bobby whenever the occasion presented itself. We were living as trivially as we did when we had bills to pay and movies to see and games to watch. Nothing had really changed. It felt wrong at times, but most of the time it felt like we were doing exactly what we were supposed to, not matter. As far as we knew, all the folks that mattered, the scientists, the politicians, the doctors, the engineers, were all dead or worse. The best we could figure is we were alive because we didn't matter. In all our travels, we didn't come across one person who made a difference in normal times. Those people seemed to be gone. Our greatest survival skill was having no skills at all. I guess sometimes it pays to have no ambition.

"Now of course Tank wouldn't agree that he didn't matter. He was a truck driver after all. Drove a big rig. Delivered everything from lumber to stuffed animals from coast to coast. He mattered.

"Never mind that driving big rigs ain't a skill that matters a lick in this world. He still thought highly of himself.

"And April was a sorority girl who made average grades and excellent excuses for all her shortcomings. Her only real skill was doing things that would make her parents ashamed and then keeping them closely guarded secrets.

"Little Bobby's uselessness was self-explanatory. He thought two plus two was penguin for hell sake, and his greatest wish was that a cartoon character was still alive.

"I was no better. I only wanted to become an electrician so I could make enough money to support my family. Seeing how there was no longer electricity , and my family was gone, I was just as useless as the rest of my band of survivors. Maybe more.

"In the middle of finding a thousand different reasons for feeling sorry for myself, I heard a swishing sound and then felt a hard whack against my ear. I reached up to soothe the sudden rush of pain. 'Ouch!' I drew my hand back. My fingertips were coated in blood. 'What the...?'

"'Arrow,' Tank said pointing to a tree in front of us. 'Get down!'

"April, Tank, and I dropped to the ground. Little Bobby approached the tree. 'Where did that come from?'

"Tank grabbed his hand. 'Get down, damn it.' He yanked Little Bobby down to the ground. 'Someone's out there.'

"We waited, breathing heavy, afraid to move. Finally, April spoke.

"'Why are they shooting at us?'

"'They don't like us,' Tank said.

"'Who's shooting what?' Little Bobby asked.

"'Shhhh,' I said.

"I could hear movement. I couldn't determine where it was coming from, but it was slow and deliberate and headed toward us. The light sound of voices muttering carried through the forest floor.

"'They're coming,' Tank said.

"Sounding panicked, April said, 'What do we do?'

"'Stay calm,' I said fighting every instinct in me to start bawling my eyes out.

"Little Bobby stood up. 'Look, people!'

"Tank reached for him, 'Get down, you idiot.'

"A sound similar to air being sucked through a straw suddenly came at us. I didn't know the source of the sound until I watched the arrow go through Tank's hand.

"Tank flopped on the ground cradling his wounded hand with the other. April screamed and crawled to the closest, fattest tree. Bobby looked on in an odd wonder.

"I jumped up. 'Hey! Stop! Please!' I realized anyone who would fire arrows first and ask questions later probably wouldn't be swayed by my use of the word please, but I figured it couldn't hurt to throw it in.

"'Who are you?' A man about fifty feet away asked. His face was painted with green and black paint. It was hard to distinguish his age. He had an arrow cocked and ready to fire.

"Little Bobby smiled and waved. 'I'm Bobby. I used to ride horses.'

"'Ahhh, don't pay any attention to him,' I said. 'We're nobody. We're just passing through.'

"'Shoot them,' a woman's voice cried out.

"'No, no, that won't be necessary,'' I said. 'We're harmless, really, I promise. We didn't know we... had violated... actually, I'm not quite sure what we did, but if you let us go, we'll try not to do it again'

"A group of six men and one woman emerged from the woods. All but the woman had arrows drawn. They wore shabby, dark clothes and their faces were covered with black and green paint.

"I turned to Tank. 'You all right?'

"He held up the hand with the arrow still lodged in it. 'What do you think?'

"'Yeah, boy!' One of the men yelled. 'Jerry got the big one through the hand.'

"'I got the puny one on the ear. Bloods still dripping,' one of the other men proclaimed.

"'Don't count,' the woman said. 'You were aiming for the head.'

"'The ear's the head,' the shooter insisted. I could tell now that he was young. Maybe mid-teens.

"'Not hardly,' the one they called Jerry said. 'That's a miss.'

"The teenager growled. 'That ain't fair. I get points for the head.'

"'You get half a point for the ear,' a man's voice replied. An older gentleman from the rear of the pack moved ahead of the others. He was taller and bulkier than the others. I got the immediate sense he was in charge. He walked over to Tank, grabbed his wounded hand and inspected it. 'Nice work, Jerry.' He turned to the young man to his left. Jerry beamed with pride.

"In a sudden graceful movement, the older man twisted the shaft of the arrow sticking out of Tanks hand and with the flick of his wrist broke it in half. Before Tank could protest, the man jerked the arrow out of Tank's hand.

"'Round 'em up,' the man said. He walked over to the boy who had been bragging about hitting me in the ear with an arrow. The older man slapped him across the face. 'Don't ever aim for the head, boy.'

"'I'm sorry, Carl.' The kid was almost in tears.

"'Sorry, nothing. You're smarter than that, Kip. We need people to tend to the compound. A man with an arrow in his head isn't going to do us much good, now is he?'

"Kip shook his head.

"Carl poked him in the temples with his thick index finger. 'Think, boy. That's all I ask.'

"Kip nodded, sweat formed on his painted forehead. He was afraid for his life. I had seen that look too many times since the world ended not to recognize it.

"The others in the group forced us to our feet and into a line. They weren't concerned about treating us delicately. Injured or not, they pushed and shoved us until we stopped struggling. I was first in line. April was behind me, followed by Bobby, and Tank brought up the rear. Our captors walked on either side of us, talking amongst themselves, but never addressing us. Tank asked them what they wanted and where they were taking us, but stopped after Carl ordered someone in his group to shut him up. One of them did so by punching Tank in the gut.

"April whimpered as we walked. She reached out to grab my arm for comfort once, but the girl in the group immediately slapped it away and told April to shut up. I looked at her and tried to muster up the courage to tell her to leave April alone, but when we locked eyes, I chickened out and quickly turned away.

"'This group seems kind of useless, Carl,' the girl said.

"'Everyone's got a use,' Carl replied. 'Whether, soldier, servant, or bait to lure in our enemies, everyone can contribute.'

"'I can do a cartwheel,' Bobby said excitedly.

"'Shut up,' Tank groaned.

"Our captors laughed. 'A cartwheel,' one of them repeated. 'That'll come in handy,' another one said.

"'Want to see?' Bobby said with an air of pride.

"With a simple raising of his hand, Carl stopped the group. He approached me. Without expression, he said, 'Shut the retard up.'

"He didn't raise his voice. He didn't have to. I got the

message. I bit my lip and stepped around April to get to Bobby.

"He had the biggest toothiest grin I hadn't seen since I found him hiding in an abandoned stable outside of Mobile, Alabama. 'They want to see my cartwheel,' he said.

"I shook my head. 'Later, Bobby. Right now you got to be quiet.'

"He didn't get it. He began to giggle excitedly. 'I haven't done it in awhile.'

"'Bobby, listen to me...'

"He held his hands above his head. 'I've got to get my hands right. That's the important part.'

"I pulled his arms down. 'Bobby, no!'

"'Leave him alone,'" April choked out between sobs.

"Carl motioned for one of his lackeys to do something to shut Bobby up. The lackey reached behind his back. I didn't wait to see what he was going to pull out. I cocked my fist back and punched Bobby in his bite wound. He shrieked in pain.

"'Shut up!' My stomach tied in knots. 'Nobody wants to see your idiotic cartwheel. You get it? You're a stinkin' retard, Bobby. Just shut up or I'll make sure the skinner dead eat you next time. You understand?'

"He was in too much pain to answer. Tank looked at me with terrified awe. In all the time we had been together, I had never flipped out like that.

"The lackey backed off. When he turned around, I saw the handle of a hunting knife sticking out of his pants. I felt a little better for what I done to shut Bobby up, but just a little.

"I turned to retake my position at the front of the line. April had stopped crying. I had either scared the tears out of her , or she had replaced abject fear with abject anger.

"Carl lifted his hand again and our band of captives and captors continued our journey through the woods."

***

"We walked for hours. Bobby never uttered another word. His silence was deafening. Each minute that passed without him speaking was a reminder of what I had done to shut him up. I told myself that it was necessary, but it never made me feel any better.

"I tried to get my mind off it by studying our captors. They were more than a gang of thugs and punks. They were disciplined. They did what Carl said without hesitation. They worshipped him. I got the feeling he could kill one of them and the others wouldn't question him. What's worse, the crueler he was the more they seemed to love him. I wasn't optimistic about our chances.

"We reached a clearing near a water inlet. The smell of sweet grass and pluff mud was almost overpowering. We were forced to break into a slow jog. Bobby stumbled and fell, but Tank quickly helped him up.

"On the other side of the clearing was an enormous house. It must have been 10,000 square feet. The front yard was as big as two football fields and nearly every of inch of it was covered in tents. There must have been three hundred of them, every size and color.

"A girl of about thirteen poked her head out of one of the tents. 'They're back!' she screamed.

"With that, hundreds of people descended upon us. They greeted their returning comrades like heroes. The chatter exploded, hugs were exchanged. A few small children ran to Carl. Their parents, or who I assume were their parents, quickly retrieved them and apologized profusely to their fearless leader for the children's behavior. He tried to smile, but couldn't quite manage.

"He watched the excitement of the others with disinterest and growing impatience. When he felt it had gone on too long, he leaned over to Jerry and whispered something in his ear.

"Jerry stiffened and quickly ran to the driveway of the house. 'Formation call! Formation call! Now!'

"The group's chatter came to a sudden halt. They hurriedly formed rows and lines until they were in a tight, clean formation standing at attention. It was apparent each person had an assigned spot in the formation and they were in place within seconds. It was amazing and frightening at the same time.

"Jerry spoke, 'Listen up, people! We left here nine soldiers strong, but we have returned with only seven. Janet and Preston died in an ambush by the Bashir. They let Carl down. He trained us better than that, and I for one am ashamed of the way my fellow soldiers died.' He turned to Carl. His eyes welling up with tears. 'I'm so sorry, Carl. You don't deserve to be disrespected like that.'

"'Please, forgive us, Carl,' the crowd said in unison.

"He raised his hand and faked a sympathetic grin. 'They were weak," he shouted. 'We are stronger for their loss!' "The crowd roared. 'We are stronger!'

"Carl caught me glaring at him with a look of disgust. For a second I thought he looked embarrassed, but then I thought better of it. He wasn't embarrassed. He was furious that I dared to look at him.

"'I've brought you entertainment.' He motioned to us, and every set of eyes focused on us. 'Tomorrow we test their usefulness.'

"A unified cheer went out across the crowd. I examined the faces of April, Bobby, and Tank. We were not as enthusiastic as the crowd.

"Carl walked to the house, and Jerry addressed the crowd. 'Break it up and get back to whatever it was you were doing. Those on kitchen duty should begin preparations for Carl's dinner.'

"Jerry approached our group, and paced back and forth in front of us. He became more and more agitated as time passed. 'You follow Carl now.' There were the telltale signs of a lump forming in his throat. His voice was hoarse and his breathing irregular. 'He is all. Do you understand me?' Tank and I shared a glance. This infuriated Jerry. He bolted forward and rammed his forehead into mine. I began to tumble backwards, but he grabbed the back of my head and pulled me toward him. 'Eyes on me, puke! I'm talking about Carl. You show him respect by listening to me!'

"April whimpered. Something she shouldn't have done. Jerry growled like a mad man and shoved her to the ground. 'Shut up!' He raised his leg as if he was about to kick her. I stepped in front of her and pushed him back. I don't know what possessed me. I'm not a hero. I had no aspiration to be one, but something I can't explain took me over at that moment.

"'Leave her alone,' I said. My mouth was dry and I clenched my fists in anticipation of putting up a meaningless fight.

"Jerry snapped his mouth shut, clicking his teeth. He looked like a wild animal about to devour his prey. I stood my ground, clenching my fists tighter.

"As I prepared to be beaten to death, Jerry's mood suddenly changed. He grinned and turned to his friends. 'This one dines with Carl. Throw the others in the pens. Get the doc to check them out. They've got a big day tomorrow.' He turned to me and lightly slapped me on the cheek. 'I hope you're ready for this.'

"Confused I said, 'Why me?'

"'Because Carl only dines with leaders.'

"More confused, I chuckled. 'I'm not the leader.'

"He smiled. 'Your actions say differently.' He reached around and grabbed April by her shoulder and pulled her to her feet. 'Otherwise, she'd have a couple of broken ribs by now.'

"April buried her face into my chest and wrapped me in a bear hug. The girl in the group pulled her away from me.

"'Don't leave us,' April begged. 'Please, Archie.'

"'Everything will be all right,' I said as the others were led away. I had a real fear I would never see them again. I never realized how much they meant to me until that moment. I vowed to myself to do everything I had to do to make sure we would be back together.'"

***

"The dining room was in pristine condition. It had none of the modern amenities I was used to, electricity or air conditioning, but it was as unfazed by the end of the world as anything I had seen before. The rest of the mansion was in disarray, but the dining room was eerily inviting.

"I sat at the head of a large dining table. Fancy china and silverware had been set around the table, twelve settings in all. I was alone for the moment. There were two entrances to the dining room, and I could hear conversations coming from both doors. Running was not an option.

"Hours passed before anyone else joined me. I had nodded off and awoke to the sound of people coming into the room. My captors, minus Carl, were among the group.

They took their seats at the table. Five other people, three girls and two boys, took the remaining seats. All of them were young. The oldest may have been my age, and I put the youngest at ten years old. They talked amongst themselves without acknowledging me.

"Carl entered and they all stood at attention. I looked on nervously, not knowing what to do. The redheaded girl to my left signaled to me to stand. I did. She smiled approvingly.

"Their leader circled the table inspecting his troops. He held a scowl until he reached his seat at the other head of the table. The group kept their eyes down. He gave the smallest smile and sat down. Only then did his soldiers dare sit. I awkwardly took my seat and grew more nervous with each passing second.

"The door to the kitchen erupted and a staff of servants filed in carrying piping hot bowls of soup. The bowls were placed in front of each dinner guest. Another team of servants filled our glasses with crystal clear water.

"No one started dinning until Carl slurped up a spoonful of his soup. The tension in the room slowly evaporated as we all ate. The soup was perfectly prepared homemade chicken gumbo. My eyes rolled back in my head after the first taste. I thought I was going to pass out it tasted so good. Bits of laughter rang out as people broke off into private conversations. Only Carl and I didn't engage in conversation with anyone. We both sat silently and ate. Freshly baked bread was brought to the table. It was warm and buttery and nearly melted in my mouth. A hint of guilt pinched my brain as I greedily gobbled up the food that was put before me. I had a gut feeling April, Little Bobby, and Tank weren't eating nearly as well. They were staying in pens after all. I wasn't exactly sure what gruel really was, but I imagined they were becoming intimately familiar with it as I ate one of the best meals I had ever had.

"The main course was rack of lamb stuffed with goat cheese over a bed of garlic mashed potatoes. It was impossibly good. After the first bite, I stared at my fork like it was a magic wand. I couldn't be experiencing what I was experiencing. I heard a chuckle.

"The redhead was wiping her mouth with her linen napkin. 'It's real,' she said. 'It's real good.'

"I was embarrassed that she had caught me staring in disbelief. I just nodded and stuffed a fork full of potatoes in my mouth.

"The dessert was a slice of caramel apple pie with a mountain of homemade vanilla cream. I was guessing it would have been ice cream if there had been any way to cool it. I ate it as if it were the last course of the last meal I would ever have and, for all I knew, it was.

"We all leaned back in our chairs and began the process of digesting the gourmet meal we had just consumed. By my calculation, it took us approximately thirty minutes to eat the entire meal, and as a result of eating so fast, every mouthful was lying heavy on our stomachs.

"Carl took a sip of water and dropped his napkin on his plate. He scanned the faces in the room. They looked away as his eyes traveled from face to face. Without warning, he picked up his plate and threw it against the wall behind my head. It shattered into little pieces.

"Everyone in the room jumped, but remained seated. 'Our existence, boys and girls, is as fragile as that plate,' he said calmly. 'I don't think you people really get that. Am I wrong?'

"No one answered, but I snickered unintentionally. The redhead looked at me and shook her head, warning me to shut up, but it was too late.

"'What's your name?' Carl asked me.

"'Archie,' Jerry answered for me.

"Carl shouted, 'I asked him!' He breathed deeply to settle his nerves. Through clenched teeth he said, 'What is it you find so funny, Archie?'

"The redhead lightly kicked me under the table. I got the message. Ask for forgiveness and hope I receive it.

"'Nothing,' I said. 'I didn't mean...' I stopped myself. I looked at the redhead and she gave me a look that reminded me of my wife. It was a fleeting look that flashed through her eyes in a split second, but I saw it and couldn't shake it. I cleared my throat. 'I... I lost...' I couldn't find the words to say what I wanted to say without making Carl even madder. 'I'm twenty-one. I know that's not very old. Although, in this room I'd say it makes me the second oldest guy here. I've seen how fragile life is first hand. I lost my family. I had a wife, a son... I had plans for the next fifty or sixty years of my life... I don't know what happened to them. I imagine what happened to them every day. I try not to, but I can't help myself.' I saw a tear running down the redhead's cheek. I smiled and turned to Carl. 'At the risk of really pissing you off, I think that telling these kids they don't know how fragile life can be is... well about the dumbest thing I ever heard. Just because they were strong enough to survive the end of the world doesn't mean they're not broken into a million little pieces like that plate.'

"The oxygen was sucked out of the room as each member of the dinner party gasped at my unabashed insolence. I had challenged the unchallengeable. I got the feeling they fully expected to see me be beheaded by the sheer will of Carl's anger.

"He sat silently, twirling his fork in his hand. His eyes fixed on me. I could feel the heat of his stare. 'Jerry,' he said still looking at me. 'Assemble everyone in the library.'

"A quick glance at Jerry revealed a seething, sweaty soldier anxious to choke me within an inch of my life.

"'Jerry!' Carl shouted.

"Jerry turned to him. 'Sir?'

"'Assemble our captains in the library.'

"Carl's second-in-command stood, eyes back on me. 'Library,' he shouted. 'Now, double time!'

"The others quickly scooted their chairs back and trotted in an organized fashion to the hallway. The redhead looked over her shoulder at me before she exited. I prayed for her that nobody noticed.

"The room was empty with the exception of Carl and me. He stood with his glass of water and moved to a chair next to mine. His posture was relaxed and unthreatening. He crossed his legs and leaned back in his chair. 'Why didn't you save your family?'

"He asked me this as if he were asking me why I let the milk in the refrigerator go sour. He didn't give a thought at how uncaring it sounded. I didn't know how to answer.

"'C'mon,' he said. 'Let's not kid ourselves. Your family's dead or worse. It's your fault. Why didn't you save them?'

"I thought I said 'I...,' but it could have been a pathetic squeak of a sound, or I may not have said anything at all. I was shocked and horrified by the question. Not because I hadn't thought about it before. I thought about it a million times a day. I didn't save my family. Whatever their fate, I was responsible. I was the husband and father. It was my job to protect them. I failed.

"'Do you want to know what I think?' Carl asked.

"I didn't but I didn't have enough wherewithal to tell him. I just sat there dumbfounded and let him speak.

"'You're not a man, Archie.'

"The tears began to fall.

"'Your little boy, what was he? Two, three years old?'

"I don't know what possessed me to answer, but I said 'Fourteen months, three days.'

"Carl laughed. 'I bet you know his age to the hour. Did he know any words?'

"'A couple.'

"'Did he know how to say Daddy?' He leaned in.

"I nodded.

"Whispering now, he said, 'I bet you even money he was calling for you when they got him.'

"I went numb.

"'Your wife, too.'

"I raised my arm and rammed my elbow into Carl's chin. His head jerked to the right and blood shot out of his mouth. He didn't cry out in pain. He brought his hand up to his face and rubbed the site of impact.

"'Nice shot,' he said hovering his head over the plate in front of him. He spat out a tooth, took a swig of water, swished it around in his mouth and spat the red fluid into the glass. He held up the tooth. 'If you want to keep on surviving this world, you got to get rid of the fragile parts that are holding you back, including those thoughts that tell you what's right and wrong, or where you failed. They don't matter. If you let them matter, you're dead.' He stood up. 'You lost your family. I don't care. Is that clear?' He didn't wait for me to answer. He moved to the door to the hallway. 'Tomorrow we see where your people fit into our group. When you get your assignments, you'll do your duties with no questions asked.'

"'And what if we don't want to join your group?' I

asked.

"I got some satisfaction when I saw him grin with one less tooth. 'Archie, it should be abundantly clear to you by know that not joining our group is not an option.' He opened the door. 'By the way, if you ever raise a hand to me again, I'll have your hand cut off.' With that he disappeared into the hallway."

***

"The redhead escorted me to the pens. I got the sense that she was ordered not talk to me, but once we were in the cover of darkness, she couldn't resist any longer.

"'My name is Madison,' she whispered. There was some awkward silence before she spoke again. 'I'm sorry about your family.' More awkward silence. 'I've never seen anyone talk to Carl like that.'

"'Yeah, well it wasn't the best idea I ever had,' I said.

"'I know he seems like a bad guy, but he's not. If it weren't for him, half of these people would be dead. The other half would probably wish they were dead.'

"'You'll forgive me if I don't throw him a parade.'

"'His methods may seem harsh...

"'I actually think it would be better if we didn't talk about... him.' I said sharply as we rounded a corner of hedges. I couldn't take her rationalizing Carl's behavior anymore. She seemed a little hurt by my tone.

"The pens were a hundred yards ahead. They were small dog pens. Tank, April, and Little Bobby where huddled together in one pen. It was maybe eight by twelve feet. There was nothing but hard ground for them to sit on.

"There were other pens. Most of them were empty, but I counted at least three others that housed people, animals, or creatures of some unknown origin inside them. There were more pens that stretched beyond the darkness. Whether they contained captives or not, I didn't know, but throughout the night we heard grunts, groans, and crying coming from the deepest darkest recesses of the pen area.

"We arrived at the door to the pen holding my crew. It was padlocked shut. Madison unlocked it and hesitated before she opened the door. 'I could talk to Carl,' she said.

"'About what?' I asked.

"Turning to me, 'Your accommodations. I might be able to get you into the house. You'd have a bed. A fully stocked kitchen to raid at night.'

"'Thanks,' I said walking past her and opening the door. 'But I like these accommodations just fine.' I stepped into the pen and pulled the door shut. The others didn't bother to greet me as I entered.

"She clicked the padlock back in place. 'Suit yourself.' She started to walk away and then stopped. 'Lose the fight.' "'What?'

"'Your first test,' she said. 'Lose.' She walked away without another word.

"'Test... fight?' I said to the darkness.

"Tank started to laugh.

"'What?' I asked.

"'Nothing. I just think it's funny that she thinks she has to tell you to lose the fight. Obviously she's never seen you fight.'

"I nodded and gave him a hard look. 'Ha, ha.' I sat across from the others with my back against the chain link wall of the pen. 'You guys okay?'

"'Super,' April said giving me the same hard look I had given Tank. 'You should have seen the lovely oatmeal they gave us to eat.'

"'They feed you?' Tank asked.

"'Ahh, yeah,' I said. 'Oatmeal. Like you.' I tapped Little Bobby's foot. 'How you doing, Little B?'

"He pulled his knees to his chest and turned away.

"'Look, Bobby, about what I did back there. I didn't want them to hurt you.'

"'You hurt me,' he mumbled.

"'They would have hurt you worse,' I said.

"'You called my cartwheel idioptic.'

"I dropped my chin to my chest and held back the urge to laugh at him. He had me there. 'I did, and I'm sorry. I was just trying to help.'

"He started picking at the chain link wall. He wasn't in the mood for a reconciliation. I backed off.

"'What did you find out up there?' Tank asked.

"I thought about his question. I learned things were getting more and more hopeless by the hour. I learned the world ended and apparently all that was left behind were cowards and jerks. I learned that given the right tools and circumstances I probably could have taken another man's life. I rubbed my chin and said. 'I learned we've got to do whatever we can to get as far away from this place as possible.'

***

"We were dragged out of the pen at first day break. A pair of lackeys I hadn't seen before threw warm water on us as we lay sleeping on the ground. They took great joy in our startled reaction to their wake-up service. They handed us bowls of cut fruit and gave us five minutes to eat it. The fruit had spoiled sometime ago, and we spit it out long before our time was up.

"They guided us through a path that took us past all the other pens. They were empty. I had the feeling the fight Madison wanted me to lose involved one of the missing occupants from the other pens.

"We passed a large oak choked by Spanish moss and entered a horseshoe-shaped bowl surrounded by small hills, lightly sloped, about thirty feet high. Carl and his followers sat on the hillside looking down on us as we approached.

"Carl clapped, 'The entertainment is here, boys and girls.' The crowd cheered.

"We were in an arena. Our first test was upon us. I scanned the crowd and saw Madison leaning against a tree at the highest point of the biggest hill. She nodded. I could read the meaning in the nod. Lose.

"Across the small field, at the foot of the hill immediately in front of us were what I could only guess were the other captives.

Only one was remotely human. And he was twice the size of Tank. The other creatures were freaks in every sense of the word. There was some kind of part ape part Délon that I would later find out is known as a Dac. There was a Bashir, and something they called a halfer that defied description.

"'Pair 'em up!' Carl shouted. 'Halfer forward.'

"One of Carl's soldiers jabbed the halfer in the back with a pitch fork and forced it to the middle of the field.

"'Let's see, who shall we pair our halfer friend with?'

"'The big one,' a member of the crowd shouted.

"'The girl,' another one shouted.

"'Yeah, the girl,' someone else concurred.

"Carl smiled. 'Ladies first.'

"One of our escorts shoved April toward the halfer. I stepped forward but was immediately punched in the kidney, which sent me to my knees.

"April tried to step back a couple of times, but each

time she was pushed forward by one of the goons. Tank dropped his head in shame. He was too afraid to do anything. Little Bobby paced nervously. He tugged on Tank's arm a few times trying to get him to help April, but Tank only responded by pulling his arm away. I attempted to stand, but couldn't catch my breath from the kidney punch.

"The halfer was poked repeatedly with the pitch fork until it couldn't take it anymore . It hobbled hurriedly and wrapped its purple arm around April's neck. She screamed bloody murder. Her only defense was to bite it, but the ugly beast seemed to take joy in her choice of defense. It picked her off the ground and tossed her aside with little effort. April pleaded for help as she crawled away from the approaching halfer. I stood despite my pain and turned to the punk who had punched me in the kidneys. I motioned for him to come closer. He witlessly agreed. As he leaned in to hear what I had to say, I gave him the same elbow to the mouth I had given Carl the night before, betting that this crony wasn't as tough as his boss. As I expected, he tumbled to the ground. I took the opportunity to turn and run out into the middle of the field. The crowd booed me. I helped April to her feet and positioned her behind me. The halfer seemed tentative. It didn't know what to do. It clumsily lunged for us, but I gave it a light tap on the shoulder and it fell in a heap to the ground. It's impractical build of half-man half-Délon obviously didn't make it very fleet of foot. It made its way to its knees and flailed wildly, grabbing for my feet, but I easily moved out of its reach. The crowd grew more and more impatient at the creature's ineptness and my interference.

"The creep I had knocked out with the elbow to the face was coming too. Happily, I watched as Tank feigned helping him up, but really struggled to keep him flat on his back. Our second escort was too occupied with trying to get me off the field to notice. I was just about ready to feel like we had won the day when I was faced with an unexpected development. The halfer's head was flattened like a pancake.

"I saw the Bashir draw back its enormous fist, its mouth open in a victory roar, strands of mucus stretching from pointy tooth to pointy tooth creating a grotesque web.

"'My opponent, I presume,' I said.

"It didn't answer. I wasn't sure if Bashirs could talk. They had a great reputation for smashing things. But they were not known for their gift of gab. It raised both fists and brought them down to the ground with an earth-shaking thud, leaving large dents in the hard ground. The force of the blow knocked me back into April and we both stumbled backward. The Bashir leaped forward and snapped its massive jaws. Its two huge tusks stopped a whisker short of the monster's black eyeballs when the mouth clamped shut.

"April screeched in my ear. The Bashir recoiled slightly from her scream. It was a promising sign. I screamed, but it had no effect. Maybe my voice was too deep. 'Scream," I said to April. She processed the request for a second and then let out a bloodcurdling scream. The Bashir cupped its massive hands over its ears. 'Again,' I said. She happily complied. The Bashir stepped back. It was working. It was too perfect to be true. 'Keep it coming,' I said, but this time she did not respond. I turned to see goon number two muffling her screams with a meaty hand over her mouth.

"I turned back just as the Bashir had made up the ground it had given and then some. The monster was just a foot or two away. Just as I was about to give up and let the smasher do its thing, I heard another scream. This one was not quite as high pitched as April's but it was a decent imitation. A glance to my right revealed Little Bobby screaming his ever-loving head off. I could have kissed him.

"The Bashir did not have the same reaction to Bobby's screams as it did to Aprils. Instead of repulsing him, the freak of nature was drawn in by Little Bobby's screeching. In fact, it even lost interest in me. It tilted its head and examined poor little stupid Bobby, and Bobby was too dumb to stop screaming.

"'Bobby,' I said. 'Stop.'

"But Little Bobby was screaming so loud he couldn't hear me. "'Bobby...'

"Before I could plead with him to stop again, the Bashir bolted toward Little Bobby. I frantically looked around for something to stop it. I spotted a baseball size rock in the field, picked it up and flung it at the Bashir. It hit the creature on the back of the head, but didn't seem to affect him at all. It stomped forward, drool hanging from its clenched mouth. Little Bobby was about to be smashed to bits and there wasn't anything I could do about it. "'Bobby,' I yelled one more time.

"This time he stopped screaming, but it was beyond too late at this point. The Bashir stopped and stood in front of Little Bobby. It nodded its massive head frantically. A clacking noise emanated from its throat. It circled Bobby. There was an unsettling sense of joy in its odd display. It was ecstatic to see Little Bobby. It craned its neck back, lifted its snout to the sky, and let out a sound like a bugle, which forced everyone in the arena to plug their ears.

"When the cry ended it was replaced with the swishing sounds of dozens of arrows flying through the air. I instinctively dove to the ground pulling April with me. I covered my head with my hands just as I heard the thwack, thwack, thwack of the arrows striking the Bashir. Most of them bounced off their target, but a few found soft spots in the Bashir's otherwise impenetrable armor-like skin. It squealed. An odd sound for such a brutish beast. Bobby stood stunned but unharmed.

"Carl and his soldiers stormed the field, new arrows drawn and ready to fire. The Bashir turned to them and snorted. It raised a fist and smashed the ground. The force of it knocked several of his attackers off their feet, their arrows flying misguided throw the air.

"The Bashir grabbed Little Bobby with its other hand and placed himself between Bobby and the unfired arrows. Little Bobby gagged. 'Archie, help!'

"I bit my bottom lip. I hoped against hope that he didn't just call my name. Why me? Tank was bigger and closer. Anyone but me. April nudged me. I rolled my eyes and slowly stood.

"'Hey... Bashir," I said.

"The grunting monster looked almost puzzled by my attempt to communicate with him.

"'Let him go.' I wanted to laugh at my own lack of leverage for Little Bobby's release. How could I possibly convince this obviously unthinking beast to release Bobby? I might as well have demanded that it recite the Gettysburg Address in pig Latin.

"'Bashirs don't negotiate,' Carl shouted as he moved to a forward position.

"'Yeah, I'm getting that.' The Bashir shifted its gaze between Carl and me. 'Any ideas?'

"'We kill it," Carl said.

"'Okay,' I said. 'Anyway you can do that without hurting Bobby?'

95

"'Probably, if we had time to formulate a plan, but time is something we don't have.'

"'What do you mean?'

"'I mean I've never heard that bugle cry before. In fact, never heard a Bashir do anything more than grunt and squeak. I got a feeling he just sent a message to his friends somewhere out there.'

"'So?'

"'So, I'm guessing the message is 'Look what I found.'

"I examined how the Bashir was holding Bobby. I could only describe it as carefully. He had no intention of hurting Bobby.

"'What's so special about, Bobby?' I asked.

"'Must've heard he does cartwheels,' Jerry said. This drew a series of chuckles from Carl's group, which did not please him at all.

"'Don't know what they want with him,' Carl said. 'Don't care. I just want to put an arrow through the thing's head before he decides to call his friends again.

"'You can't. You might hit Bobby.'

"'Not my biggest concern right now,' Carl said. 'I just want to keep a herd of these big uglies from knowing our little community's location.'

"'But...'

"The Bashir raised its head in preparation to let out another bugle call. Carl pulled back on the string of his bow and instructed his soldiers to do the same.

"'Wait, wait, wait,' I said 'Don't...'

"Before I could finish, the Bashir let out a garbled bark. I turned to see it fall face first to the ground. An arrow was sticking out of its ear.

"On the top of the hill, still standing where she was when we entered the little arena, Madison lowered her bow.

"'Ease off, men,' Carl barked. 'Nice shot, Maddy.' He pulled out a large hunting knife and approached the Bashir. 'That didn't go as planned,' he said kneeling down.

"'You had a plan?' I asked.

"'Of sorts,' he said as he jammed the knife in the Bashir's arrow-free ear making a sickening, slicing sound.

"'What was your plan?'

"'Maybe they were more like expectations than a plan.' He pulled the knife out and cleaned the blade on his pant leg.

"'Okay,' I said. 'What were your expectations?'

"'That the Bashir would pound you into raw meat.'

"I swallowed hard.

"'Don't take it personal,' he said. 'That's the way these things usually go, but for some reason the Bashir took a keen interest in Mr. Cartwheel.'

"Little Bobby examined the dead Bashir with great interest. He was fascinated by it. More so than I think I had ever seen him.

"'Well,' I said, 'I once heard that animals go after the weakest in the group.'

"Carl laughed. 'Son, to the Bashir we're all the weakest. And just because this thing isn't human doesn't make it an animal. No, sir, there's something more to it than that. The Bashir wanted Bobby. That sound it made. He was telling all his friends he found something... maybe something they've been looking for.'

"Bobby tapped Carl on the shoulder. 'Excuse me, Mr. Carl, but can I have the claw?'

"Carl looked at him perplexed. 'What claw?'

"'The Bashir's claw. I need it.'

"Carl shook his head. 'Bashir's don't have claws, Bobby.' He returned to our conversation. 'I'm not so sure it was a good idea bringing you all into our camp.'

"'Wait a minute,' I said. 'We didn't exactly come here by our own free will.'

"'Well, you're here now so I can't let you leave...'

"'Yes they do," Little Bobby said.

"'What?' Carl barked.

"'Have a claw.' Bobby leaned down and picked up the Bashir's heavy arm. 'See,' he grunted. There was a pouch on the underside of the wrist. Bobby pushed the tough fleshy hide beneath the pouch and a razor-sharp claw shot out like a switchblade.

"'I'll be a...' Carl started as he leaned in to examine the claw. He peered up at Little Bobby. 'How did you know it was there?'

"'That's where it's supposed to be,' Little Bobby answered.

"'What does that mean?' Carl asked.

"Bobby shrugged his shoulders. 'Can I have it?'

"Carl nodded and slit the pouch open with his hunting knife. With some effort, he cut through the Bashir's arm and removed the claw. He handed it to Little Bobby.

"'Thanks,' Little Bobby said. 'This will help a lot.'

"Carl stared at Bobby for several seconds. 'I don't like this.' He turned to the punk I had knocked out earlier and said, Take them back to the pens.' He walked to the middle of the field. 'The tests are cancelled for today.' The crowd groaned with disappointment. 'See your duty sergeants ASAP for your day's assignment.' The crowd immediately began to disburse. 'Captains!' Carl barked. 'The library in five!' He stormed off without another word."

***

"They put us in separate pens after the incident at the arena. They truly didn't know what to do with us, and I guess they thought that keeping us apart was the safest course of action. We could still see each other and carry on conversations, but we couldn't huddle together and seek comfort in the closeness of each other.

"Little Bobby curled up in his pen holding onto the Bashir's claw. He was asleep shortly after they padlocked his pen door. He had a strange smile on his face as he snoozed the late morning away.

"The rest of us were pensive to say the least. Tank paced stooped over in his pen. April rocked back and forth hugging her knees to her chest. I picked at the ground and tossed scraps of dirt and grass into a little pile in front of me. We didn't speak to each other for a long time. It may have had something to do with the other captives being so close by, but I think it was more that we were afraid of what we might say.

"Tank was the first to break the silence. He stopped pacing and propped himself up with his hands on the chain link wall of his pen. 'You ever catch your old man in a lie, Archie?'

"I looked at him puzzled. 'What?'

"'My old man was in Vietnam. He used to talk about it all the time. The stuff they did. Not the bad stuff you read about in books and see in movies. The good stuff... acts of bravery, you know?'

"'Yeah,' I said.

"'By the time I was ten I thought the only difference between Superman and my dad was that Superman could fly.' He sat down. 'Then one day I caught my old man in a lie. I can't even remember what it was. Something small. Lied to my mom about how much he spent on something, I think. My mom was pretty tight with the dollar. She had the old man on a short leash when it came to the household budget. He was scared to death of her when it came to spending money.'

"'People lie,' I said. 'Some lies are bigger than others, that's all.'

"'I know,' he said. 'I get that. But I started thinking about all his war stories. All those brave things he'd done. What if those were lies, too?'

"'Just cause he lied once doesn't mean he lied all the time,' April interjected.

"Tank shook his head. 'It was more than once. I started keeping count of the lies he told. He lied a lot.'

"'C'mon, I think you're reading too much into it. I'm sure your dad was a good guy,' I said.

"He nodded. 'He was. I'm just not sure he was the guy I wanted him to be. The guy in those stories he used to tell. I want to be like that guy. If he lied about that, then that means I want to be a lie.'

"I thought about what he said and finally asked, 'It doesn't matter how much your dad lied anymore, does it?'

"'Does to me,' he said.

"'Well, it doesn't to me,' I said sounding too much like Carl.

"'What's that supposed to mean?' Tank asked.

"'It means the world where your old man told lies is dead! It's over! It's gone! Along with every stupid little insignificant lie he told. Be your own man, Tank! Stop moaning and crying about the man your dad wasn't and be the man you want to be! That's what matters to me and April and Little Bobby. Got it?'

"He gave me the same look he'd given me when I punched Little Bobby in his bite wound. 'You're a real jerk, you know that, Archie?'

"I kicked at the pile of dirt and grass I had created. 'Yeah, I guess I am.' I could feel myself losing my cool so I turned away from the others and closed my eyes tightly. I wanted this all to be a bad dream. Maybe if I closed my eyes long enough, I would open them and the world wouldn't be this turned upside down crazy mess that it was.

"I opened my eyes at the sound of Little Bobby screaming. Two of Carl's goons had come down from the mansion and were pulling him out of his pen.

"'What are you doing?' I asked. 'Leave him alone.'

"Tank started pulling on the chain link wall of his pen. 'Hey, get your hands off him!'

"'Let go,' Little Bobby screamed. 'I don't want to go! Archie!'

"'Hey, hey, fellas,' I said. 'C'mon, have a heart.'

"The goons ignored us.

"'Stop them,' April pleaded with me.

"'Take me,' I said. 'I'm the leader remember? Take me.'

"Tank violently jerked on his chain link enclosure. 'I'm going to rip your head off!' he barked.

"The goons chuckled at this threat. One of them said, 'Carl wants to see him do a couple of cartwheels, that's all.'

"They jostled Little Bobby and pushed him past the pens. I slapped the side of my pen. 'If he gets hurt, I'm holding you responsible.' Upon hearing that, one of the goons slapped Little Bobby on the back of the head hard enough to make him cry out in pain.

"They disappeared around the corner. Madison appeared shortly after they had gone.

"'Bring him back, Madison,' I said.

"'He'll be all right,' she said. 'Trust me.'

"Tank laughed sarcastically. 'Trust you? Sure, okay. You kidnap us and lock us in cages and we're supposed to trust you.'

"'We're just trying to protect the community,' Madison said. 'You want to help him. Tell me everything you know about him.'

"'What's to tell?' I said. 'He used to be a jockey. He's a little slow. I found him in Alabama. Mobile. He's harmless.'

"'Why would the Bashir be so interested in him?' she asked. "'I don't know and neither does Bobby. You're wasting your time if you're trying to get any information out of him.'

"'It's the bite!' April said.

"'What?' Madison said walking over to her pen.

"'The skinner dead bite. We were attacked by some skinner dead and one of them bit Bobby. That's it. The Bashir smelled the bite. That's all," April said with such confidence that I was willing to accept it as an explanation.

"'Doubtful,' Madison said. She turned to me. 'You fought off some skinner dead?'

"I looked at Tank and April before I answered. 'We got away.'

"'Impressive,' she said. 'They've taken out more than a few of our own.'

"I hung my head. I didn't have the heart to tell her that they would have gotten us all if it weren't for Lou.

"Madison leaned in close to me and said quietly, 'I'll do what I can to protect Bobby, but you gotta tell me everything you know.'

"'I have,' I said.

"She sighed deeply. 'All right. Try not to worry. If the Bashir see a value in Bobby then so does Carl. He's not going to do anything to jeopardize that.'

"'Yeah, well Carl doesn't exactly strike me as the most rational guy on the planet.'

"She smiled. 'Bobby will be okay.'

"I shook my head. 'I don't get it. You're not like the others. You see through Carl's crap. I can see it in your eyes. Why are you so loyal to him?'

"This time she dropped her head. 'He's my father.'

"Shocked by her revelation all I could say was 'Whoa.'

"She nodded. 'Bobby will be fine.' She turned on her heels and walked back to the house.

"'You trust her?' Tank asked.

"I looked at him for a long time before I answered. 'I don't know if I trust anybody.'

"He nodded. 'Me either.'"

***

"It was nightfall before we saw anyone else from the community. Jerry and the two goons who took Little Bobby entered the pen area and unlocked our doors. They didn't talk. They just stood and waited for us to exit the pens on our own. We did so reluctantly.

"With no verbal communication at all, Jerry and the other two directed us to the front yard of the house. The entire community had gathered around a huge bonfire. The crowd parted as we entered. Carl and the rest of his captains stood near the flames. We approached tentatively. I scanned the area for Bobby, but he was nowhere to be found.

"'We sent out a scout team after your test today,' Carl said.

"'Where's Bobby?' I asked.

"'I've trained my people well,' he said ignoring my question.

"'Congratulations. Where's Bobby?'

"'The scout team is made up of some of my best.'

"'I don't care about your scout team,' I said. 'Where's

Bobby?'

"'I sent them looking for any signs of Bashir.'

"'Terrific! Where is Bobby?'

"'They didn't find any Bashir, but they did find this.' He stepped back, and somebody was shoved forward. It was a girl. Her disheveled chestnut hair covered her face. She brushed it back and I saw Lou's bruised face looking back at me.

"I stepped forward, but Jerry grabbed my arm. I tried to work myself free of his grip, but I was grabbed by another one of Carl's goons.

"'A friend of yours?' Carl asked.

"'We've met,' I said.

"'She doesn't talk much.' Carl grabbed a handful of her hair and yanked her head back.

"'Take it easy,' I said. 'She's just a kid.'

"'Kid?' Carl laughed. 'Charlie, Randy, Melissa, front and center.' Three battered and beaten members of Carl's community stepped forward. 'Meet my scout team.'

"I held back a smile. 'She's still just a kid,' I said.

"Carl shoved her forward and let go of her hair. Lou stumbled and landed at my feet. I helped her up.

"'You okay?' I asked.

"She winked.

"'This has gone too far now,' I said. 'You should let us go. We'll take Bobby and get out of here.'

"'Lou!' A voice cried. I turned to see Madison escorting Bobby from the front porch of the house. 'It's Lou. It's Lou. She saved me from the dead people.'

"Carl scratched the back of his neck. 'It's true you people have proven to be quite the liability.'

"'Then let us go,' April pleaded.

"'Can't,' Carl said. 'You know where we are.'

"'Hey, genius,' Tank said. 'If you're so worried about keeping this place a secret, why do you have a bonfire shooting flames twenty feet into the air?'

"Carl admired the fire. 'Beautiful, isn't it? But it's not for show. It's for protection.'

"'Protection?' April asked.

"'The lung locusts are coming tonight.'

"'Lung locusts?' I said looking at Lou to see if she knew what he was talking about. She turned away. Not a good sign.

"'We call them that, but to be honest we don't know what they really are. They come by the billions. They fill the sky. Black out the night. And they come every sixty-three days. There's so many of them that you can't help but breathe them in. They fill your lungs, and you drown in locusts.'

"'Gee, that sounds fun,' Tank said. 'Why don't you just go in the house?'

"'They get in the house. This is the safest place. We only lost five people last time, but they were the draws.'

"'The draws?' I asked.

"'The locusts are drawn to blood. We post five people on the farthest points of the property to draw most of the locusts away from us. The fire protects us from the rest.'

"I did the math in my head. With Lou, our group was now five members strong. 'Five, huh?' I said.

"Carl smiles. 'You catch on quick. Takes care of two problems for us. What to do with you and who we're going to sacrifice as draws.'

"'Wait a minute,' Tank barked. 'No... you can just forget it. I'm not standing out there waiting... to be swarmed by...'

"Carl laughed. 'You didn't really think we were going to ask you to volunteer. I'm afraid you have no choice in the matter.'

"'You think I'm just going to stand out there and let those things...' Tank started.

"'Again,' Carl said. 'You underestimate us. Your accommodations have been arranged.'

"'Accommodations?' Tank said.

"April shrieked. We all turned to see her frantically raking her hands through her hair, and hopping around like she had suddenly gone insane. 'Get it off! Get it off!'

"'Get what off?' I ask.

"A single locust flew out of her hair and landed at my feet. 'That!' she screamed.

"Carl walked over and picked up the insect. 'A scout.' He tossed it into the fire. 'Get the draws to their posts!'

"Jerry grabbed my arm and started to escort me to my post, but we were stopped by Madison. 'I can't take the retard anymore. Let me have this one,' She said to Jerry.

"'But Carl put me in charge of this one,' he answered.

"'Jerry, we don't have time to argue.' She pried my arm away from him and handed him Bobby's arm. Jerry hesitated and then took hold of Bobby. 'You're taking the heat from Carl if he gets pissed.'

"'Deal,' she said, and began to roughly escort me to my post. She looked over her shoulder a few times to make sure we weren't being followed. Finally she spoke. 'Here.' She handed me the Bashir's claw. 'I can't give you a knife because Carl knows every knife on the compound. If one goes missing, he'll do whatever it takes to find out who took it. This should cut through the ropes.'

"'What about the others?' I asked.

"'I can't do anything for them and, if you try, the locusts will get you. In about ten minutes, visibility will be almost zero. We won't be able to see you from the bonfire. Cut your ropes and run.'

"'I can't leave my friends.'

"'You have to.'

"'Would you?'

"We reached a ten foot post. 'Doesn't matter what I would do.' She put my back against the pole and tied my hands together. 'I have to make this tight,' She said. 'I'm sorry. I wish I could do more...'

"'Maddy,' Carl barked. 'Who authorized you to switch with Jerry?'

"'No one, sir. I just couldn't take that retard anymore.'

"Carl rapidly approached. I cupped my hand around the Bashir claw. He stepped behind me and yanked on my ropes. Satisfied, he peered at Madison as he stepped toward her. Without a word, he backhanded her across the face. 'My orders are never to be altered again!'

"She reached up and massaged her cheek. 'But, Daddy...'

"He hit her again. Through gritted teeth he said, 'Don't ever call me that. I'm not your father. I'm your leader.' He pulled her knife from the sheath on her belt. Holding it in front of her he said, 'Cut him.'

"She took the knife. Her eyes on him, she slashed the blade across my ribcage. I felt the cold sensation of the blade followed by a searing heat. I fought not to cry out in pain.

"He eyeballed her a few more seconds and then walked off to inspect the other draws.

"'Wait until you can't see the fire,' she whispered. Tears were flowing freely down her red cheeks.

"I could see Jerry tying Little Bobby to his post, but I couldn't see the others. 'Where are the others?'

"She sighed. I could tell she was fighting with herself. Part of her didn't want to tell me, but the other part of her knew she had to. 'The posts are fifty yards apart. They stretch all the way to the inlet. Just keep heading east.' She started to walk away, but stopped. 'If you try to save the others, you'll all die.'

"'Maybe,' I said. 'But if I run, I won't be able to live with myself anyway, so I don't have anything to lose. Why are you helping me?'

"She smiled. 'Because I don't have anything to lose.' She turned and ran to the bonfire.

"The next few minutes were eerily quiet. Other than the roar of the fire, there wasn't a sound. I could see the silhouetted figures of the members of the community swaying back and forth in front of the flames. The silence was broken by a sudden low rumbling thunderous buzzing. I looked up at the sky and watched a black curtain shut out the purple nightglow. It was impossible to make out individual locusts because they flew in such a tight formation. I started to cut away at the ropes. It was difficult to get my hands in position , and I almost dropped the claw at one point. But once I got the claw in position, I sawed away at the rope at a breakneck pace. Little by little, the fire and the silhouetted ghost community began to vanish. The rope snapped strand after strand as I cut through it. I tugged with all my strength and broke free from the post. I slipped in the dirt as I headed east toward the next post. Stumbling forward, I placed my hand on the ground and lost my grip on the Bashir claw. The light was totally gone. The claw was only out of my hands for a second, but it might as well have been lost to me years ago and miles away. I couldn't find it. I fumbled through the thick grass, mumbling to myself, 'Please, let me find it. Please.' My hand ran across something sharp. I winced in pain and nearly cried tears of joy. I picked up the claw and called out, "Who's there? Where are you?" The buzzing locusts grew closer and closer.

"'It's me,' Little Bobby yelled. 'Why?'

"I followed the sound of his voice and ran into him almost at full speed. I succeeded in knocking the breath out of myself, but I held tight to the claw.

"'Heyyyy,' Bobby gagged. 'You hit me.'

"I felt in the darkness for Bobby's hands. 'Stand still.'

"'Archie?' he said. 'It got dark.'

"'Yeah, I know,' I said as I cut away at the rope.

"'What are you doing?'

"'I'm trying to cut you loose.'

"Bobby's rope was easier to cut than mine. I freed him in a matter of seconds. 'C'mon,' I said grabbing his hand. We ran screaming in the darkness. When someone screamed back, we headed toward the sound of the voice and found Lou. As I was cutting her rope, I felt a locust smack me in the head followed by another and another. We freed her and again cried out for the next person to give us their location while we ran through the darkness holding hands. April was next. Lou held on to Bobby while I cut through April's rope. I could feel the locust crawling all over me while I cut with a frenzy I had never known before. April yelped in pain as I accidentally cut her hands. 'Sorry,' I said.

"'Don't be sorry,' she said spitting a locust out of her mouth. 'Just cut!'

"I freed her and we ran into the darkness screaming for Tank. He barked. 'Here! Here! Here! Hurry.'

"We reached him and I quickly started to grope in the pitch black for the ropes that bound him. He was almost entirely covered in locusts. I swatted them off his arm and began to cut the rope. He coughed and hacked. 'Hang on, Tank.'

"'Forget it, Arch,' he said. 'Just get out of here.'

"'Shut up," I said. 'I've cut through four ropes with

this thing. I'm starting to get the hang of it...' I heard a snap, and my hand slipped forward. The claw had broken. 'Crap!'

"Tank laughed. 'Don't tell me.'

"'What?' Lou asked.

"I couldn't bring myself to say it out loud. 'Help me get these ropes untied,' I said.

"She felt for my shoulder in the darkness and then fumbled in the darkness until she found Tanks hands. We both started to tug on the ropes. There were a bundle of knots, and we couldn't tell which way was which. April and Little Bobby began to cough violently. The locusts were getting thicker and thicker.

"'Go!' Tank said. 'Get out of here!'

"'We're not leaving you," I said. I could feel the locusts crawling in my nose. I snorted them out, blowing snot and locusts all over Lou.

"'Listen,' Tank coughed. 'It don't make sense for four people to die trying to save one broken down truck driver.'

"'Stop talking,' I said pulling on the knots. 'I can't concentrate...'

"Bobby's coughing got worse with each passing second. I grabbed Lou's hand. 'Get them out of here,' I said.

"'He's right,' she said.

"'What?'

"'Tank's right. We have to leave him.'

"'I'm not...'

"'You know he's right!' she said.

"'Let's go," April cried.

"'Go,' Tank said.

"I screamed like I had never screamed before. I jerked the rope one last time. 'Tank... man... no.'

"'Go!' he demanded. 'Before I break free from these ropes and beat the crap out of you.' He laughed and coughed.

"Lou dragged me for the first ten feet until I shook loose from her grip and ran ahead of the others into the thick covering of the woods. I cupped my hands over my ears so I couldn't hear Tank choking to death."

EIGHT

"We wandered throughout the night. It took us hours before we couldn't hear the buzzing of the locusts anymore. We were picking the nasty little bugs out of our hair and clothes longer than that. I would shudder occasionally as I remembered the sensation of the locusts' prickly little feet crawling across my bare skin. I couldn't get them out of my mind.

"I began to plot my revenge against Carl the second I made the decision I couldn't save Tank. He would pay for Tank's death. I would make sure of it. It was now my one and only purpose on this crap-hole of a planet. I would make him suffer just like Tank suffered. Of that I was nothing but sure.

"We stopped at dawn in a clearing near a muddy creek. I let the others sit before I chose a spot as far away as possible without losing sight of them. I didn't want to socialize or to talk about what had happened or to cry over our friend Tank. I wanted to think about what I was going to do to Carl. I wanted to get mad and madder still. I wanted time to hate what he had done, what he had forced me to do. I wanted to plan my revenge in detail. I couldn't do that with April whining about how tired she was or Little Bobby crying about how he missed his horses. I couldn't do that with Lou and her ridiculous fantasies of

Storytellers and Keepers and Takers and the great warrior Oz.

"I sat under a large Cyprus tree and began to develop my plot to kill Carl. The others must have sensed my need to be alone because they didn't even attempt to join me. I guess they could have been cooking up the same schemes I was cooking up. I looked over my shoulder and saw Little Bobby snoozing away with April's arm draped over his shoulder. She sat, eyes drooping, fighting the need to sleep herself. She saw me looking her way and managed a half-hearted smile before she broke out in tears.

"I heard footsteps approaching from the creek. I swiveled my head around so fast I heard my neck pop. I was both relieved and angry to see Lou standing a few feet away. She bent down and propped her forearms on her knees while weaving her fingers together. She stared without speaking.

"I let it go on for several seconds before I finally spoke. 'What?' I said angrily.

"She cleared her throat. 'You're a creyshaw.'

"'I'm not in the mood, Lou.'

"'No,' she said. 'You're really a creyshaw. A warrior.'

"I laughed. 'I don't feel like playing warrior today...'

"'Listen to me. You are a warrior. You have a Keeper to find. You have a Storyteller to protect. Canter wasn't just making an offhanded remark. He literally meant that you are a creyshaw.'

"I tried to soak in what she was saying, but I couldn't get the sound of the locusts choking the life out of Tank out of my head. 'Go away, Lou. Leave me alone.'

"She sighed. 'You lost your friend. I get that. It's tough. I've...' She hesitated and breathed in deeply. 'I've lost people, too, but we don't have time for you to cry for Tank.'

"'Lou, shut up!' I barked. 'Leave me alone.'

"'No!' she barked back. 'You don't get the luxury of feeling sorry for yourself. You're a warrior. You understand? This isn't a joke. It's not a game. It's a freaky little world where the purple people are losing control day by day and they'll do anything to get it back. I need you to man up and take this seriously.'

"'I don't want to be a warrior!' I tried to convey the depth of my anger with a penetrating stare, but she gave it back to me and then some.

"'Want?' she chuckled. 'I want to be in Disneyland with my brother and grandparents enjoying the happiest place on earth, but that ship has sailed, my friend. Wants aren't on the agenda anymore. You're a creyshaw. You have a duty and if you don't carry it out this world will keep on getting worse and worse until we'll all be just as dead as Tank.'

"I stood. 'Read my lips. I don't care.'

"I heard her joints crack as she stood. 'Wait a minute.' I ignored her. 'What if I told you there's a possibility we can go back?'

"'Back where?' I asked still walking away.

"'Back to our world. Before all this began.'

"I stopped. Turning, I said, 'Before...?'

"'Yes.'

"I nearly fell to the ground. I couldn't believe my ears. 'We can go back?'

"'I don't know,' she said. 'I used to think so. The further I get from who I used to be, I'm not so sure anymore, but Oz believed it. He thought it was possible.'

"'How?'

"'I told you I don't know. But the Destroyers want the Storytellers so I figure it's got something to do with them.'

"'Tell me how this works,' I said.

"'The Storytellers created the Destroyers. They underwent some kind of therapy and training by this doctor in Buffalo. He taught them to create things with their minds. They suffered from Down syndrome. So they used their talent to create hell on earth to punish all the people who tormented them.'

"I thought about what she said. I looked at Bobby. *Down syndrome*, I thought.

"'Yeah,' she said. 'I heard Carl's thugs talk about how the Bashir acted toward Bobby.'

"'Do you think...?'

"She shrugged her shoulders. 'There might be a way to find out.' She walked past me and headed toward Bobby and April. She whistled. 'Hey, wake up!'

"April snapped to and Bobby groggily lifted his head.

"'C'mon,' April said. 'Please don't tell us we have to keep going. We're tired. We need to rest.'

"Ignoring April, Lou addressed Bobby. 'You ever hear of HMI, Little Bobby?'

"Bobby looked down. He shook his head.

"'What's that?' April asked.

"'Hyper Mental Imaging,' Lou answered. 'It's kind of like magic, isn't it Bobby?'

"Bobby backed away from her and pressed against April.

"'What's wrong, Bobby?'

"'What was the doctor's name?' Lou said. 'The one who taught you to make things with your mind. Dr. Baker?'

"'Dr. Bashir,' Bobby said. He immediately covered his mouth with his hands.

"Lou smiled. 'Of course. Dr. Bashir.' She looked at me. 'That's why he called his monsters the Bashir.'

"'No,' Bobby said shaking his head. 'It's not my fault.

It's not my fault.'

"'What's going on?' April asked.

"Lou gently touched Bobby's arm. 'We know. Dr. Bashir made you make the monsters. Didn't he?'

"Bobby nodded. 'He was a mean man. He liked to hit. He made us think bad thoughts. He wanted us to hurt people.' "'It's all right, Bobby,' she said. 'We're here to help you.'

"'Not you,' Bobby said. He pointed at me. 'Him.'

"I stepped back. Every instinct I had told me to turn and run and never look back, but I was terrible at following my instincts. I swallowed and said, 'Why me?'

"'You were nice to my horse once,' he said.

"'I looked at him dumfounded. 'What are you talking about, Bobby? We didn't know each other before...' I lifted my arms and spread them wide. 'This.'

"'Yes we did,' he smiled.

"'No we didn't. I found you in Mobile.'

"'The second time,' he said. 'The first time you found me in Birmingham.'

"I thought about what he said, and suddenly realized it was a real possibility I had seen Bobby before. I had been to a horse track in Birmingham. Years ago. I was a kid.

"'You came to the track,' he said. 'You told your friend my horse was smarter than me.'

"'That's it?' I said. 'You chose me because I said your horse was smarter than you.'

"He shrugged his shoulders. 'Everyone else thought my horse was kind of dumb. But you didn't. You believed in him.'

"I waved my arms and walked away. Lou ran after me. 'Where are you going?'

"'He chose me because I was nice to his horse. I wasn't even being nice to his horse. I was making fun of him. I'm not the guy. I'm not the warrior. It's somebody else.'

"'That's the way it works. The people who are the creyshaw, the warriors, they weren't chosen because they were ideal citizens. They were jerks... Most of them.'

"'What about Oz? Was he a jerk?'

"'The biggest,' she said. 'But I figure that's what this is all about. Bad people getting a second chance.'

"'I'm fine with who I was. I don't need a second chance. I was a kid when I said that about Bobby. I'm supposed to pay for that now? Besides he doesn't even think it was a bad thing.'

"'I don't have all the answers. All I know is the Bashir are coming after Bobby. Like it or not, you're the only one that can save him.'

"I dropped my shoulders and lifted my chin to the sky. 'This is ridiculous, Lou. I can't stop the Bashir.'

'Not alone,' she said.

"I turned to her prepared to laugh in her face. It would take an army a hell of a lot bigger than me and her and April to protect Bobby. But when I looked her in the face, I saw a determination that was impossible not to believe. She could save the world with one hand behind her back. I shrugged. 'Okay, I'll save Bobby.'

"She smiled. 'Great! Now all we need is Ajax.'

***

"Much to April's dismay, we rested for only thirty more minutes before we continued on. Lou had set up a checkpoint with her crew. She was already a few hours overdue thanks to her abduction by Carl's goons. They wouldn't wait much longer for her. They had to keep on

117

the move or they were at risk of being caught by the Délons. She believed purple creepies were on the hunt for Oz and, as far as they knew, he was wherever Wes and Lou and the others were. And if he wasn't, he would come for them if he thought they were in trouble. And he would, but Lou had no idea where he was. He had left a year ago to find the Source, the key to the Délons return to absolute power.

"That's why Lou formed an alliance with the Silencers. She promised them the Source if they helped her find Oz. She had no idea what or where the Source was, but she convinced them that Oz knew, and she could get him to turn it over to the overgrown crustaceans. They agreed and fed her the latest tips on Oz's whereabouts, all the while keeping the Délons distracted and off her back. But she was growing more and more mistrustful of the Silencers and knew it was just a matter of time before their agreement was ended and she and the others were turned over to the Délons. She was running out of time, and so was Oz. I didn't want to ask her what made her think he was still alive. I knew she had thought about it. It was written on her face when she talked about him, but she had an unflappable faith that he was alive because I'm sure he promised her they would see each other again. That's the kind of thing people said to each other even though they had no way of keeping the promise.

"After walking and talking for an hour, April finally piped up. 'This is crazy! You people are just going to have to stop. My feet hurt. I'm about to collapse from exhaustion. And I'm pretty sure Little Bobby's been asleep on his feet for the past couple of miles.'

"'We can't stop,' Lou said. 'C'mon it's not much farther.'

"'I don't believe you,' April said. 'You're just saying that. I'm not stupid, you know...' Her jaw dropped and her eyes opened wide. She stumbled backwards while pointing behind me.

"I turned to see a large white hairy monster marching through the woods in front of us. It was fifteen feet tall, with a broad mouth and red eyes.

"'Tarek,' Lou said excitedly. She ran to the beast and hugged it tightly.

"'Lou,' it said in deep explosive tones.

"'It's been so long.' She reached down in some thick brush and picked something up. I saw legs dangling around her hip. She was holding a child. One of about two or three wearing a tiny little backpack. 'He's getting so big,' she said.

"Tarek spotted us and approached. 'Who's this?'

"'I found another warrior and Storyteller,' she said.

"It sniffed the air. A needle-toothed grin spread across its ugly face. 'Indeed,' it said. 'You are indeed.'

"'How do you know?' I asked.

"'I know things,' it said. 'Your name?'

"'You don't know?'

"'Would I have asked if did?'

"'Archie Maynard.'

"It reached down, wrapped its enormous hand around me, and lifted me up. 'You aren't much.'

"Lou shook her head. 'He says that about all the warriors.'

"'Well,' Tarek said. 'None of them are much. It's frightening to think the future of your world is in the hands of something as puny as this creature.'

"'You want to put me down?' I said having a little trouble breathing.

"Tarek effortlessly tossed me aside. I went tumbling to

the ground nearly crashing into April and Bobby. I winced in pain as I stood and brushed the dirt from my clothes. April stared at the white monster with extreme trepidation, while Bobby seemed oddly calmed by Tarek's presence.

"Tarek lost interest in me and watched Lou holding the child. 'This one is already trouble. He is into everything.'

"Lou tweaked the youngster's nose and made him giggle. 'It's tough being a parent,' she said.

"Tarek shook his massive head. 'A Keeper does not a parent make. I am his protector. It is not my job to raise him.'

"'Gee,' she said. 'Whine much?' She bounced the child on her hip. 'Why are you here anyway?'

"'He's begun,' Tarek said. 'The stories.'

"Lou stopped bouncing the kid. 'It's too early. You said it would take him years.'

"The giant beast shrugged. 'I was wrong. Look in the backpack.'

"Lou put the child on the ground and unzipped his backpack. She removed a piece of paper from it and straightened it out. I could see it was a drawing, a rudimentary one at that. It appeared to be a large nondescript black mass. Meaningless.

"'What is it?' Lou asked.

"'You can't tell?' Tarek replied.

"'A ball?'

"'It's a cave," Bobby said and then immediately looked away sheepishly

"'Bingo,' Tarek said.

"'A cave?' Lou said. 'How do you get a cave out of this?' "'I don't,' Tarek said picking up the kid. 'But he does, and that's the important thing.' He walked to the thick forest canopy from which he emerged.

"'What does it mean?' Lou asked.

"'Not sure yet,' Tarek said, 'but I'll keep you posted. Incidentally, Wes and the others are about a half mile south of here.'

"'Bye, Nate,' Lou cooed. 'See you soon.'

"'By the way, Archie Maynard,' Tarek said. 'At the count of three, you will be wide-awake and feeling better than you did before.'

"'What are you talking about? I'm not asleep.' I looked at Lou for confirmation that I was indeed awake, but she was gone.

"'One, feeling refreshed and confident.' Tarek said. "'Two, feeling revitalized and ready to have a productive day. Three, open your eyes. You're wide awake, rejuvenated with a clear mind.'

Oz

NINE

Bones is waiting for me when I emerge from the closet. He begins to speak, but I cut him off before he gets the second syllable out. I am tired. I am angry. I am confused. In other words, it is business as usual for me in this place. I thought listening to Scoop-face's sessions would give me answers, and if not answers, hope that I wasn't completely off my rocker, that the things I thought happened really did happen. But so far, all I've been able to determine is that Scoop-face is as crazy as me.

Bones is surprised as I pass the hallway to my room and continue on toward the rec area and cafeteria. I am not in the mood to sit and stew in my room and go over the story Scoop-face is spewing in his sessions. Bashirs, militant survivors, lung locusts. That didn't happen. And if his story is clearly nuts, then my story is obviously nuts, too.

I groan. Not in frustration, but in relief. I am nuts. The Takers, the Délons, General Roy, Reya, Ajax the talking gorilla, none of that is real. I know that now. The memory of them can't haunt me anymore because it's not a memory.

They are serving ice cream in the cafeteria. I think I haven't had ice cream in a very long time. I know I haven't because the second I see it, I want to eat an entire gallon... no, not want – I need to eat an entire gallon.

I have not been in the cafeteria before. I hear spoons clank against porcelain bowls as I make my way to the ice cream line. Most of the crazies watch my every move. They are unnerved by my presence. They don't know what to make of my visit. I stand behind the fat lady who is scared by her own farts. I pray she doesn't let one go. Bones is standing behind me. He is unsure of my motives. He has been instructed to watch over me, but he has no idea how to protect me from myself.

"Ah, chief," he says. "Do you think it's a good idea to be here?"

"I'm hungry," I say. "You don't have to stay."

"It's just that..." He smiles nervously at our onlookers. "You're kind of freaking everyone out, and believe me, boss, these aren't the kind of people you want to freak out."

"Do I make you nervous?" I yell out to the crowd.

"Oh, geez," Bones mutters. "Shhhhh, you can't... stop drawing attention to us."

"Why?" I ask the cafeteria. "We're all crazy here. I know I am. I just found out today that my second hand doesn't go all the way around the clock, if you know what I mean."

Bones backs away from me. "Whoa, whoa, whoa, shhhh." He turns to the cafeteria. "He's okay folks. He's just making conversation. Back to your food. I'm sure it's delicious."

I step up to the metal counter with the wait staff looking at me like I have three heads. "Scoop of vanilla and chocolate, please," I say.

"I don't like this, boss," Bones says. "I really don't like this."

"Then don't get any," I say.

"That's not what I mean," Bones says. "We should be back in your room. Archie will be around to see you tonight. You might want to sit and think about what you're going to say to him."

The lady behind the counter hands me my bowl of ice cream. The mounds are perfectly scooped. They look like works of art. I sit at a nearby table and hesitate. It feels wrong somehow to destroy such perfection. I quickly shake it off and cut through the chocolate mound with my spoon. I let the ice cream touch my lips first. I savor the feel of it. The smell of it. I cannot believe how relaxed it makes me. I shove the spoonful of ice cream in my mouth and close my eyes. It is heaven. My next spoonful is vanilla, then chocolate, then vanilla. I alternate the two flavors with an ever-increasing pace. I feel the cold racing through my veins until a pounding pain hits me between the eyes. Brain-freeze. I double over. Eyes shut tight. I press my thumb and index finger against the bridge of my nose. I grow dizzy from the pain. The muttering from the others grows louder and louder. My eyes still closed, I can feel them closing in on me. I hear a tray crash to the floor.

"Oz," a voice echoes through my throbbing head. I am in too much pain to respond. "Oz." I breathe rapidly, sucking air in deeply and pushing it out through pursed lips. The pain begins to slowly subside. I feel the muscles in my body begin to relax. I open one eye and then the other, fluttering my eyelids to adjust to the light. The fluorescent glow of the cafeteria is gone. There is now a faint yellow radiance above my head from a single light bulb hanging from a vaulted ceiling.

"You're wasting time," a voice says.

I stand. "Who's there?"

I hear the click, click, click of spiked feet approaching. Canter steps under the yellow dome of light. "This is getting us nowhere."

"What are doing here?"

"Failing to make you see the truth," he says.

"Which is?"

"You're crazy."

I laugh, softly at first and then I cackle madly. "I know I'm crazy. Where have you been?"

He shakes his upside down head. "You've accepted it temporarily. It will pass. Eventually you will start to believe again. Archie will get to you. He'll convince you that you are a warrior... a great warrior who is the key to vanquishing the Destroyers. But you're not. Do you understand me? You've done bad things. You've killed people... people you love." He points down.

I look at my feet. Lou lays bleeding. I'm stunned beyond words. I begin to hyperventilate.

"It's not true," I hear Scoop-face say. He steps out of the darkness led by Bones.

I hear Canter scream in my head. "How did you get in here?"

Scoop-face smiles. "I found your hiding place," he says. "That's the benefit of getting in somebody's head."

I bend down and stroke Lou's cheek with the back of my hand.

"Do you remember her real name," Scoop-face asks.

"Shut up," Canter says. He rushes Bones and Scoop-face, but stops short. Bones shields his face with his left arm.

Scoop-face smiles. "Relax, Bones. The Silencer is harmless here."

"Her real name," I say to myself.

"Lou is just a nickname," Scoop-face says. "If you can remember her real name, you can go back."

I turn to him. "Go back where?"

"Back to the cave. Before the shunter. You made a mistake. You can correct it."

Canter chuckles. "There is no going back."

"The cave?" I shudder at the sound of the words. Why would I want to go back there?

"If you can remember Lou's real name. You'll find her. You can correct your mistake and get back on the right path. The Storytellers want you to win, Oz, but you have to figure out how on your own. They want to give you a chance to do the right thing."

"Storytellers," Canter sneers. "They are weak and feebleminded. They have no power because they chose corrupt and undeserving warriors to save the world."

Scoop-face smiles. "That's the problem with you Destroyers. You never understood the power of forgiveness."

Canter rolls his eyes. "Please." He stomps a single spiked foot and the light bulb that illuminated the room explodes. "And you humans never understood the power of darkness."

***

I awake in my room. I shake the cobwebs and feel strangely refreshed. As I swing my legs over the bed and rub the soreness out of my shoulders, I hear the dead scatter. I can't bear to seek them out. I know they are there. That's enough.

I peer up and see something on the padded wall in front of me, a word... no, two or three words. I narrow my eyes and try to focus on them. I can't see them through the gloom. I stand and slowly shuffle towards the wall. I am afraid and curious at the same time. I have a desire to know what it says, and I have a fear that knowing will harm me in some way. When I make it out, I realize that it did more than harm me, it confused me. Written in blood is "Millie B. Story."

***

Scoop-face arrives in my room an hour later. His eyeless face is highlighted by an impossible smile.

"What are you smiling at?" I ask.

"I don't know," he says. "I guess it's just good to get back there. To see everybody again."

"Everybody like Tank," I say.

His smile disappears. "There was nothing I could have done."

I shrug my shoulders. "Didn't seem like you tried very hard."

A scowl now. "I guess I'm not the great and powerful Oz."

I sigh. I feel bad for what I said. "I don't want to do this anymore, Archie. I belong here. The world is better off with me in here."

"The world would have been better if you were a good person. We're here because of you. You can't decide to quit. You are creyshaw!"

I laugh. "You see! That's it right there! The whole creyshaw business! It's nonsense!"

"Keep your voice down," he says. He whispers. "You have to see this through."

I wave him off. "There's nothing to see through. It's not real."

"It is," he says raising his voice. "It has to be." He points to his face. "How did this happen to me?"

"I don't know. Maybe you were born like that for all I know." He stomps. "No, think. You know. You were there. You did this to me."

I examine the vacant area of his face, and try to absorb what he just said. I couldn't have done that. "What... me?"

"Think," he demands.

I try to recall what he wants me to, but I can't. "Why would I do that to you?"

"Because I asked you to," he says.

I snicker. "Now I know you're crazy. Why would anyone want that done to them?"

"Because if you didn't, I would have become one of them. I'd rather have no face than become one of them."

A flash of a memory pops off in my brain. I see the shunter on Archie's face. My fingers are digging deep into the jellyfish body of the face-sucker. I am pulling it off with all my might. Archie is holding on tight to my arm.

The memory gone, I fall to my knees. "I did that to you."

He puts his hand on my shoulder. "Warriors make hard choices. That's what makes them warriors. You are creyshaw. You have to see this thing through."

I nod. "I am creyshaw." I force a laugh. "You should know that I'm more coward than warrior."

He makes his way to the door. "We all are."

***

When I arrive in the janitor's closet the next afternoon, I discover a pen and small notepad sitting on one of the supply shelves. I grab it and flip to a blank page. I write down *Millie B. Story* and then tap the pen on the paper just as I had seen Dr. Graham do a thousand times. I write down *Lou's real name?* She told me. I know she did. I examine the name *Millie B. Story*. The harder I stare, the more the letters float apart.

Archie enters Dr. Grahams office and their session begins.

Scoop-face

TEN

"'I'm sorry to hear about Tank,' Wes said. 'He was good people.' The portly former auto mechanic was tinkering with the engine of his VW bus.

"Lou pulled her finger out of a jar of peanut butter and stuffed it in her mouth. In spite of that, she tried to speak. 'Really good guy. We could have used him, too.'

"I was eating some fresh baked flatbread. It was hard and barely edible, but I was hungry enough to marginally enjoy it. Valerie had made it for us, and I didn't want to be rude by not eating it. I don't know why I was holding on to the old social norms, but I couldn't let them go.

"'This community they took you to,' Wes said. 'You sure you weren't followed?'

"'Nah,' Lou said. 'The locust gave us cover. They're probably just now figuring out we got away. They'll send out search parties, though. They're afraid we'll give up their position.'

"Ajax huffed and grabbed the jar of peanut butter from her. He dug his finger into the sweet sticky treat and pulled it out. He sniffed it and hooted with delight. He sucked the peanut butter off. I wondered how much he could enjoy it without a tongue, but it didn't seem to hold him back at all.

"'Nice,' Lou said with a disgusted look on her face. 'Keep it.'

"He happily complied. Kimball sat next to him at full attention. Ajax smacked a glob of peanut butter on his canine friend's snout. Kimball's tongue shot out of his mouth and frantically attacked the gooey treat.

"'We should attack them while they're not expecting it,' Tyrone said.

"'Attack?' I said.

"'We're not attacking anything,' Lou said. She pulled the drawing that Tarek had given her out of her pocket and handed it to Wes.

"'What's this?' he asked.

"'Saw Tarek and the little guy,' she said.

"'Did you now?' Wes said.

"Valerie squealed. 'How is Nate?'

"'Growing like a weed. He drew that,' she said pointing to the drawing Wes was holding.

"'Let me see,' Valerie said taking the drawing from Wes. "The old mechanic scratched his cheek. 'He's taken to drawin' has he?'

"Ajax suddenly became interested in the conversation. He dropped the jar of peanut butter and quickly moved next to Valerie. Kimball pounced on the abandoned jar.

"Ajax peered over Valerie's shoulder at the drawing. He turned to Lou and signed something to her. She smiled and nodded.

"'That's right,' she said. 'Cave.'

"'Told you,' Little Bobby said.

"'Oh, yeah,' Valerie said. 'I see it.'

"'No you don't,' Tyrone said. 'You're just saying that.'

"'I do too,' she barked.

"'Don't you two start up again,' Wes groaned. 'I've had it up to here with your bickering.'

"Ajax signed some more.

"'We will,' Lou said.

133

"'We will what?' I asked.

"'Find the cave.'

"'What cave?' Wes asked snatching the drawing from Valerie.

"'This cave?' He turned the drawing around and showed it to Lou. 'It's a brown and black blob. This isn't a cave. It's scribbling by a kid... a kid who's... you know... slow.'

"'He's a Storyteller, Wes. He's trying to tell us where Oz is. I know it.' Lou took the drawing from Wes and carefully folded it.

"'Well when you see a cave that looks like a crayon threw up on the side of a mountain, you let me know,' Wes said. He turned back to the VW bus and resumed his maintenance of the engine.

"'I know where it is,' Little Bobby said.

"We all turned to him.

"'Of course,' Lou said. 'He's a Storyteller.'

"'Wait a minute,' I said. 'Let's not get ahead of ourselves, here.' I had been traveling with Bobby for weeks. He had boasted about hundreds of exploits that were in retrospect probably not true. I even doubted his stories of racing horses. He clearly worked with horses in some capacity because that's where we had first met, but as far as him ever racing them, that was most likely a lie. I didn't want Lou to get her hopes up. I didn't know much about Storytellers, and what they were capable of, but I knew Bobby better than anyone left on the planet. I wouldn't put a whole lot of stock into anything he said.

"But it was quickly apparent that I could have given Lou a thousand reasons not to believe Little Bobby, and it wouldn't have done any good. She had made up her mind. Bobby was the answer to finding the cave, and if we found the cave, we found Oz. I went back to chewing my almost unchewable flatbread and hoped that Bobby was telling the truth. I had never met Oz. I had only heard stories of him from Lou and Tyrone and Valerie, but I found myself wanting him here. This creyshaw thing was beginning to freak me out. It carried a lot of responsibility, and I wasn't sure if I would ever be up to it. If I failed, the Destroyers gained even more power. I could use a mentor and as far as I could tell, Oz was the warrior for the job.

"Lou sat and interrogated Bobby. I should have listened, but I wanted a break from hearing what lay ahead. I stood and walked to the rear of the VW bus where Wes was working on the engine.

"'Can I talk to you?' I asked.

"He looked up. 'What's on your mind?'

"'Oz,' I said.

"Wes stood erect and wiped the grease from his hands with a filthy rag. He raised an eyebrow. 'What about him?'

"I cleared my throat. 'Well, as far as I can tell, he's the only warrior that's succeeded. He got his Storyteller to his Keeper.'

"'So far,' Wes said.

"'Yeah, so far,' I agreed.

"'And?'

"'How did he do it?'

"Wes smiled. 'Because he's a warrior.'

"I shook my head. 'I don't know what the means.'

"Wes leaned against the VW bus. 'A warrior doesn't fight for himself.'

"'I know that. They fight for the Storytellers...'

"'No,' Wes said. 'That's just the end result. A warrior fights to undo a wrong, whether he created the wrong or not.'

"I kicked at a tree root in the ground. 'I'm not much of a fighter. In fact, I've run from just about every fight I could.' I hesitated before I went on. 'I hid out.'

"Wes shrugged. 'Hid out?'

"'In my garage. When... they came through our neighborhood. I heard them in my house. I knew my wife and son were in there, but I didn't do anything to save them. I froze. I let them take my family.' I sighed deeply. 'I've never said that out loud before.'

"Wes chewed his bottom lip. 'Then I'd say you're the perfect warrior.'

"Perplexed," I asked, 'Why?'

"He lifted himself off the VW bus. 'Because you definitely have some wrongs to undo.' He went back to fiddling with the engine.

"'Thanks,' I said sincerely.

"'For what?' he asked without looking up.

"'For not telling me what I did was normal. That anybody else would have done the same thing.'

"He looked up, thought about a response, and then just simply nodded.

"My head hung low, I walked away and looked for a spot to sit and think. I scanned the small clearing and marveled at how relaxed the atmosphere was. April was braiding Valerie's hair. Tyrone looked on with a childlike wonder at April's skill. Ajax and Kimball were playing. Lou was questioning Bobby. Everyone had a place. They fit perfectly as if this was always supposed to be. A knot formed in my stomach. If I had agreed to join Lou and the others back at the greenhouse, Tank would still be alive. I had made a decision that cost another man his life. I had a lot of wrongs to undo.

"I sat on a fallen tree at the edge of the clearing and thought about the day I hid in my garage. I tried not to, but the memory forced itself upon me. I couldn't hold it back.

136

***

"The wind swirled outside my bedroom. It carried a driving rain that pelted thick droplets of water against the window. I watched it with an unusual interest. Birmingham had been without electricity for three days at the time, and I was bored beyond belief. My son was asleep, and my wife and I had talked until we didn't have anything new to say to each other. So I watched the rain. I was amazed at the power with which it struck the glass. There were times I was sure a crack would develop from the pressure of the hit, but one never appeared. Each raindrop made its own unique sound against the window, whack, thud, pop, thwack.

"My wife was the one who suggested I go into the garage and get a board game to pass the time. She sat on the edge of the bed with me and found the rain less fascinating than I did. She sat with her chin on my shoulder and tried to share my enchantment, but she couldn't take more than two minutes of it before she suggested we play Monopoly or Trivial Pursuit or whatever, just anything but watching the rain.

"I resisted at first. I was in a peculiar trance that made me feel more relaxed than I had felt since the world had come to an end. I didn't want to give that up. But she insisted, jokingly at first. She playfully punched me in the arm, nibbled my ear, pinched my side. She finally pushed me with a force that suggested that she was doing more than proposing that we play a game to pass the time. She was insisting that we play a board game to make our lives somehow normal again.

"I stood in a huff and said something harsh, more harsh than I intended. She was hurt by my reaction. She had no idea how precious that last moment had been to me. There was no reason she should have. I wasn't the type of person to share my feelings with other people, not even my wife. There was no one on the planet I was closer to, but I didn't want to burden her with the up and down nature of my moods. I pretended to be happy when I wasn't. I pretended not to worry when I did. I pretended to be strong when I was far from it. Pretending was something I did very well. It was my greatest talent.

"I exited the bedroom, immediately missed the rain, and quickly headed for the living room on my way to the garage. I could get a look at the rain from that window. It was on the backside of the house and it would give me a different view point. When I reached the window, I was surprised to see the rain had picked up in intensity. It was coming down in sheets. I could barely make out the world outside the house. I peered through the waterfall of rain and saw a group of people standing in my neighbors', Harriet and Jim Compton's, yard. Their features were distorted by the blurry perspective of the water-covered glass. I counted a dozen people dressed in black. I put my hands on the window and formed a tunnel to try and focus on the group. Two of them were dragging something. I wiped at the glass, but it did nothing. A pulse of rain washed away a clear spot, and I could make out what they were dragging. Harriet Compton.

"I backed away from the window and dropped to the floor. My heart was racing. I scooted backwards to the wall. A black shape passed outside the window followed by another and another. I pushed myself along the floor against the wall, scurrying to get out of view if someone should look in the window. I turned the corner of the wall and pulled myself up. The front door rattled. I peeked around and saw the doorknob moving. I looked around for a weapon, anything, even if it was a thick book or a rolled up magazine. Nothing. I breathed in. I told myself to exhale and make a dash for the bedroom. The group of invaders started to push against the door. They would break through at any second. I had to act quickly. I took a half step forward and heard the wood panel of the door splinter and give way. I turned and saw the door to the garage. I couldn't do it. I couldn't just leave my wife and child to fend for themselves.

"I tried to will myself to turn back around, but I saw my hand reach out and grab the doorknob. I tried to pull it away, but I had no control of my body. Quickly and quietly I opened the door and moved into the garage. They were in the house. I could hear them muttering amongst themselves. I ran to the water heater and settled in behind it, wedging myself between its cold metal frame and the unfinished garage wall.

"I closed my eyes when I heard my wife scream, and I covered my ears when I heard my son cry. I never once found the courage to even stand. I prayed they would find me so I would pay for my cowardice, but they never even looked in the garage. I sat there and listened to them drag my family out of the house.

***

"Ajax and Lou approached me in the mid-afternoon. I had fallen asleep somewhere along the line, but it was a restless and pointless sleep. I wasn't exactly refreshed and ready to carry on a conversation with a fifteen year-old girl and 400-pound gorilla.

"'We need to talk about our next move,' Lou said.

"'You people have done this before," I said through a yawn. 'I was counting on you to tell me what to do.'

"Ajax went through a series of signs.

"'Ajax thinks we should head for the high country. There's a band of gorillas that can help us.'

"'Gorillas?' I said. 'Like him?'

"Lou nodded and watched Ajax sign something. She smiled. 'He says there's only one Ajax, but there's a colony of apes in the mountains of South Carolina, a place called Saluda. They may be able to help us find your Keeper.'

"'Any chance they've got a phone and we can just call?' I asked with a smile. They didn't respond. 'Not even a banana phone, huh?' Again no response. 'Okay, Saluda, here we come.'

"Wes joined our group. 'We're going to have to walk it. The VW has finally kicked the old bucket. For the best, really. It was getting harder and harder to find a clear road to travel.' He looked over his shoulder at the little bus. 'Still, she did her part. Gotta say that for her.' He choked back a tear.

"Lou caressed his arm. 'It's not going to be the same without her.'

"I snickered louder than I intended. Lou glared at me. 'Sorry,' I said.

"Wes returned the snicker. 'I know it's stupid to get all choked up over a car, but it was the last thing we had that was the way it used to be.'

"I looked at the fat little van and felt like a heel for not seeing it before. I had no right to make fun of them. They were saying goodbye to more than a car. They were saying goodbye to their old lives.

"'So,' I said. 'Just how far is this Saluda place?'

"Wes sniffed and gave the question some thought. 'I'd say about 270 miles or so.'

"I looked at Ajax. 'Don't suppose you got any gorilla friends any closer.'

"The ape shook his massive head and hooted.

"'Never hurts to ask,' I said. 'Without a car, that'll take some time.'

"'If we can get in a good solid eight hours of walking a day, it should take us nine days,' Wes said. 'But that ain't taking time for trouble into account. I'd say we should be there in two weeks, three weeks maybe.'

"'Three weeks?' I groaned. 'What kind of trouble are you expecting?'

"'It'd be easier to say what kind of trouble I'm not expecting,' he answered.

***

"The next morning we all gathered around the green and yellow VW bus. Wes gave her a pat and thanked her for her service. Valerie kissed her hood and Tyrone gently tapped the front passenger-side tire with his foot. Lou gutted her of all the supplies. She handed out weapons to everyone: crossbows, knives, fireworks. No guns. I had learned myself that at best they only worked occasionally and at worst something could go terribly wrong and blow your hand off. Wes took this as another sign that the Délons were losing control. I hadn't noticed until now that Lou was without the sword she'd had when we first met.

"'Lost it to those creeps back at the community,' she said when I asked her about it. 'I'll get it back. You can count on it.'

"'You think we'll run into them again,' I said hoping the answer would be yes.

"'Please, I've seen jerks like Carl before. He's got too much ego to just let us slip away.'

"'Good,' I said.

"She grabbed my arm. 'The best way to screw this

thing up is to let revenge get into the way of your job. Got it?'

"I nodded, but I didn't mean it. She knew it, too, but she let it go.

"'April,' she yelled.

"April looked shocked at hearing her name called. She quickly walked over to us. 'Yeah?'

"Lou handed her a crossbow and a quiver of arrows. 'You're taking point with me. From now on, you're going to have on-the-job training.'

"'Training for what?' April asked.

"'War,' Lou responded nonchalantly.

"April handed the crossbow back to Lou. 'No thanks. I'll just be the designated cook or something.'

"Lou rammed the crossbow into April's chest. 'We all cook. We all fight.'

"'Ahhh, no,' April said with her best Southern drawl. 'I don't fight, okay. I'll do the girl stuff.' She dropped the crossbow on the ground.

"Valerie and Tyrone started to giggle. Wes propped his foot up on the bumper of the now defunct VW bus and smiled. Even Ajax and Kimball looked on wide-eyed. They were all enjoying this. I felt a need to intervene.

"'Maybe she's right,' I said to Lou. 'I don't think she'd be much help in a fight.'

"Lou looked at me crossly. 'Did you not hear me use the word training?' She removed an arrow from the quiver around her shoulder.

"'In case you haven't noticed,' April said. 'I'm older than you. You can't tell me what to do. I'm in college... or I was.'

"'Fine,' Lou said loading the arrow into the crossbow. 'You want to do girl stuff?' She pointed the crossbow at April. 'Then you'll do girl stuff.'

"'Lou, what are you doing?' I asked.

"April held her breath and raised up on her toes. 'Don't shoot. Don't shoot.'

"'Put the crossbow down, Lou,' I said. I stopped short of stepping between the razor sharp arrow and April. 'Please.' The others watched with the same amused expressions they had before. Only Little Bobby seemed as concerned as April and me.

"Without saying another word, Lou pulled the trigger. I watched with a morbid curiosity as the arrow headed straight for April. She stood frozen in time. The arrow zoomed through her hair and struck something in the woods directly behind her. I heard a pained squeal as a Dac collapsed to the ground with the arrow sticking out of its throat.

"Lou tossed the crossbow to April. 'Walking point. Killing Dacs and anything else that's not human, that's girl stuff, clear?'

"April stood with her mouth open in an 'O' shape. She swallowed, hugged the crossbow she'd once rejected, and nodded.

"Tyrone jumped up in the air. 'Nice shot, Lou!' He ran over to the fallen Dac. 'Fox Dac,' he said. He pulled a notepad out of his pocket and wrote something down. 'That makes three.'

"'Four,' Valerie shouted. 'There was that one in Winchester.'

"'That was a cat Dac,' he said.

"'No it wasn't,' Valerie responded. She joined Tyrone standing over the slain Dac. They continued their argument in quieter tones.

"I felt obligated to say something comforting to April and approached her with every intention of doing so, but when I reached her all I could think to say was, 'I guess girl stuff ain't girl stuff anymore.'

"'She could have killed me,' April whispered.

"I watched Lou stuff some supplies into a backpack. 'Yeah, she could have.' I walked away feeling stupid for ever wanting to give her words of comfort.

***

"We covered a little more than thirty-five miles that first day, and Wes was pleased because that put us ahead of schedule. We had left the cover of the woods and traveled north on highway 174. Cars and trucks of every make and model littered the cracked pavement. Even if the VW bus had been running, it would have been impossible to drive on the route we had decided to travel.

"I cooked that night, beans and some canned meat. It tasted like it sounded, disgusting, but it was a warm meal. None of us were complaining. Everyone scarfed down their food like they hadn't eaten in days.

"Lou tossed her tin plate aside and leaned against an abandoned Toyota Corolla. She twirled her head around to loosen the kinks in her neck. It was one of those rare moments she looked her age. There was an innocence dancing from her eyes that I had never seen before. She pulled the drawing of the cave out of her pocket and studied it. Suddenly it dawned on me. She had hope. It had been hiding in her somewhere until now. The scribbles of brown and black crayon on the wrinkled piece of paper brought it out of her. I wondered who this Oz was. Really. I knew he was a warrior or creyshaw, whatever you want to call it, but as far as I knew he wasn't a superhero. Why did she put so much faith in a guy she hadn't seen in a year?

"I ate one last spoonful of beans and set my plate on the hood of an Escalade. I picked a couple of pieces of black licorice Twizzler twists out of my backpack. I had found the candy under the seat of the VW bus. Wes begged me to take the treats off his hands. It seems he couldn't stand licorice. I gladly obliged him. It was one of my favorites.

"I joined Lou by the Corolla and offered her the extra Twizzler. She took it with a smile and tore off a chunk of the candy with her teeth.

"I pointed at the drawing with my licorice twist. 'You really think we can find the cave based on that drawing?'

"She chewed her candy. 'I wouldn't still have it if I thought it was useless. Besides Tarek thinks we can use it, otherwise he wouldn't have given it to me.'

"I stuck my Twizzler in my mouth and sucked on it. The licorice taste was almost spiritual. I bit off a chunk. 'Oz means a lot to you, doesn't he?'

"'He means a lot to all of us. He's the...'

"'The key. I know. I've heard, but that's not what I'm talking about. He means more than that to you.'

"She blushed slightly. 'What do you mean?'

"'Look,' I said. 'It's all right, okay. I understand how you feel.'

"'Feel about what?' she asked.

"'Oz. You love him,' I said.

"She howled with laugher. 'Love him. Are you kidding me?'

"'You don't have to be embarrassed.'

"'Oz Griffin is a turd. I do not love him. I'm not old enough to love somebody, and if I was, it wouldn't be him, I can tell you that. He's a big jerk.' She was getting angrier by the minute.

"'All right, all right, you don't love him. I'm sorry.'

"'Why would you say something like that?' she asked.

"'Clearly, I wasn't thinking straight. My bad.'

"'We need him. He can end all this.' She stood and threw what was remaining of her Twizzler to the ground. 'Love, please. The first thing I'm going to do when we find him is give him a big fat lip for leaving us like that, all this time. Not a word. Making us worry half to death. I wouldn't ever love somebody who's that big of a horse's ass.' She stomped off muttering to herself.

"Valerie popped up from the other side of the Corolla with a big smile on her face. 'She is so in love with him.'

"'Obviously,' I said.

"I heard a gravelly grunt as Ajax raced past the Corolla. Kimball was on his heels. I stood to see what interested them so much. Dusk was making its way through the purple sky. I watched as Ajax and Kimball bolted down the road toward the violet horizon.

"A single Silencer approached.

"Wes unwittingly startled me as he stood just to my right and said, 'Rogue.'

"'What?' I asked.

"'Only one Silencer travels alone and that's Canter. We got us a freelancer.'

"'And that's bad?'

"'That's bad.' He turned to Valerie. 'Lil' bit, you and Tyrone load up. Crossbows. Take positions on both sides of the road.'

"Valerie ran to get Tyrone.

"'What do we do?' I asked.

"'We try to talk our way out of trouble.'

"We started walking toward the Silencer. 'If that doesn't work?'

"'If that don't work, we kiss our alliance with Canter goodbye and kill the freak,' Wes said.

"'Nobody's killing anyone,' Lou said walking past us. 'We need Canter. Let me handle this.' She trotted toward the Silencer. Ajax and Kimball had already stopped the Destroyer from getting any closer.

"'I don't get it,' I said. 'If this guy's a freelancer, why would Canter care if we took it out?'

"'You're right,' he said. 'You don't get it. We're on the bottom of the food chain. In Canter's mind, one Silencer's life is worth a million human lives. Don't matter if the Silencer is rogue or not. Canter will help us in a fight or feed us information to defeat the Délons, but we kill a Silencer and he'll bring all hell down on us.'

"Lou held her arms out to show the Silencer she didn't have any weapons. The beast towered over here. She grabbed Kimball by the scruff of the neck, pushed him back, and then quietly begged Ajax to behave with a few signs. I couldn't hear the Silencer's part of the conversation. It swayed and bopped its upside-down head. Lou put her hands up and urged the monster to stay put. She ran back to us.

"'He just wants to pass,' Lou said.

"'What's he doing out here by himself?' Wes asked.

"'He says he's a messenger for Canter. He's carrying a message to a colony of Silencers a couple of days walk from here.'

"'He's lying,' Wes said. 'I ain't never seen a Silencer travel alone.'

"'Look,' Lou said. 'He just wants to pass. Let's let him through, and that'll be that.'

"Wes rubbed his chin. 'All right, but the young ones aren't putting down their crossbows.'

"She nodded. 'Agreed.'

"She raced back to tell the Silencer he could pass. I could tell by Wes's face that he was going against his best judgment. He put his arm around me and pulled me in close. Whispering, he said, 'Don't say a word. If the

Silencer hears your voice, he'll get a bead on your brain waves. They can get inside your head if you ain't careful. We got an agreement with Canter. He stays out of our head as long as we help him out. But I bet good money this one here ain't holding to any such agreement.'

"I nodded. 'What about Lou?' I whispered.

"He snickered, 'They's in for a world of hurt if they get inside her head.'

"The Silencer moved toward us, its eyes scanning from left to right as it walked. It reached the Corolla and as a show of strength pushed the small Japanese car out of its way rather than walk around it. Wes and I quickly stepped back to avoid getting hit by the vehicle. The Silencer plowed forward. It snapped its head to the right and peered at Valerie. It stooped at the waist and eyeballed her.

"This incensed Ajax. The Gorilla leaped on the hood of the Corolla and let out a tongueless roar followed by a frantic beating of his chest. The Silencer turned to the great ape and narrowed its eyes. Kimball bared his teeth. His fur stood on end. Our two warriors from the animal kingdom were on the verge of pouncing.

"Lou stepped between them and the Silencer. 'Get out of here before I change my mind,' she said.

"The Silencer leaned in closer to Lou. She bent backwards. Ajax climbed to the roof of the car. It began to buckle under his weight. The situation was about to explode.

"'You heard her,' Valerie cried. 'Get moving.'

"The Silencer quickly turned its attention back to Valerie. It stared at her. It reeked of smugness. It was hard to say why. Maybe it was the sound of Valerie's voice, but it was clearly pleased. The half-man half-crab passed without further incident. As I watched it walk out of sight, I couldn't help but feel that Wes's instincts were right. We should have killed the freak.

***

"Wes cleared out the back of the Escalade, collapsed the back seats, and laid out on the plush leather. He was mad at Lou and didn't speak five words to anyone after the encounter with the Silencer.

"Valerie had spoken fewer words. She had been unnerved by the Silencer. I could only assume that it was because it heard her voice and got inside her head. She kept her distance from the rest of us, and we all sensed she needed some time alone. Ajax and Kimball kept a vigil over her, backing off only when she screamed at them to leave her alone.

"'What do we do?' I asked Lou.

"Lou shrugged her shoulders. 'Let the cry baby sulk.'

"I gave her a disapproving glare. 'That's a little rough.'

"'What do you want me to do? Stroke her hair and tell her everything will be all right?' Lou pushed past me. 'You go coddle her if you want to. Or send your silly sorority girl April over there. I'm not in the mood to kiss it and make it feel better.'

"'You know, not everyone is as heartless as you, Lou. You need to learn how to make nice.'

"She disappeared behind a small U-haul truck.

"'It got in her head, too,' Tyrone said from atop a Honda Element. 'She won't admit it, but it did. The farther that thing gets away from here, the better they'll get. You'll see.'

"I stood at the front of the Element. 'There's nothing we can do?'

"He shook his head. 'Leave 'em alone is about all you can do.'

"'I don't feel right leaving Valerie out there in the dark all by herself. She's too far away.'

"'Ajax and Kimball will keep her safe, and I got a good view of her from up here. This ain't our first night sleeping out under the stars,' he smiled.

"I smiled back. 'Guess not.'

"'I'm going to marry her, you know,' Tyrone said blushing. 'Not for a while, but someday, when we're old, like twenty or something. I already asked her.'

"'She said yes?' I asked.

"'She said if I'm not as big of a creep when I get older then maybe. But she doesn't really think I'm a creep. She likes me.'

"'You're pretty sure about that, aren't ya?'

"He shrugged his shoulders. 'I guess.'

"I tapped the hood of the Element. 'Make sure you invite me to the wedding.' I left to check on April.

***

"I awoke to the sound of a thundering crash. I opened the door of the minivan I had chosen to sleep in and stumbled out onto the pavement. Ajax and Kimball joined me as we headed toward the sound. Ahead of us, Wes, Tyrone, April, and Lou stood in front of a pick-up truck. It was bouncing up and down. A heavy street bike was sticking out of the truck's windshield.

"'What happened?' I shouted.

"Wes turned with a bewildered expression on his face. 'It's the damndest thing. It looks like this motorcycle dropped out of the sky. Smashed the truck all to hell.'

"'Motorcycles don't just drop out of the sky,' I said.

"Tyrone looked over our group. 'Wait a second. Where's Valerie?'

"A scream rang through the night as Valerie's name left Tyrone's lips. We all turned to see her being lifted into the air by the Silencer had we had let pass earlier.

"'Valerie!' Tyrone shouted.

"We all bolted after her.

"The Silencer crab-walked to the edge of the road holding Valerie above its head and jumped into the dark cover of the woods.

"'Weapons,' Wes yelled. We all stopped to collect them except Tyrone, Ajax, and Kimball.

"'Tyrone,' I said. 'Wait.'

"He didn't listen. He reached the spot where the Silencer disappeared into the woods and did the same. Ajax and Kimball were right behind him.

"I looked at the woods that bordered the road. It was pitch black past the tree line. My whole body began to shake. I had doubts that the courage that had eluded me when my wife and child were taken would suddenly make an appearance in order to save Valerie. I closed my eyes and searched the recesses of my mind for something to help me shake the overwhelming fear. Nothing came. I felt someone brush past me.

"'Move,' Lou shouted.

"I opened my eyes to see her and Wes heading for the woods. I heard a twig snap to my right. I made out the Silencer's head as the monster moved rapidly through the forest. I held a crossbow and then dropped it when I realized I had never fired one before. I couldn't take the chance of firing at the Silencer and accidentally hitting Valerie. I bent down and picked up a large hunting knife. I gripped the handle tight.

"I tore through the woods to my immediate right and pursued the Silencer. The others were nowhere to be seen. My guess is that they had gotten lost in the darkness, exactly what the Silencer had planned. He hadn't counted on a coward who lagged behind because he was too afraid to immediately jump into action.

"It wasn't long before I had him back in my sights. He had slowed to a walk. I slowed too.

"'Hey!' I shouted.

"The Silencer stopped and turned. He no longer had Valerie.

"'Where is she?' I demanded.

"I felt him smiling. It was a frightening feeling of dread and morbid satisfaction. Valerie was dead. He nodded as he read my mind. 'I gave her to my parasites once I got what I wanted.' He held up a fist wrapped around a severed tongue.

"I felt the blood rushing through my body. 'She was just a kid.'

"'They have the sweetest tongues.' He shoved the tongue into a slit on his neck. He closed his eyes in ecstasy.

"I let out a scream that sprang from my gut and poured out in long deep tones. I had never heard such a sound come out of me. I rushed the Silencer. It crouched. I felt my brain vibrating as I got closer. I heard Wes's word of warning repeating in my head, 'they'll get in your head.' I stopped in my tracks and dropped the hunting knife. I placed my hands on my head and squeezed, trying to stop the vibration. I spun around and fell to my knees. I felt as though I would vomit. I placed a hand on the cold ground to prop myself up. Movement in the distance caught my eye. Skinner dead feeding. The Silencer's parasites. I closed my eyes and saw myself hiding in my garage, listening to my wife screaming and my son crying. Not again. I picked up the knife and stood.

"'You want in my head?' I said.

"The Silencer laughed. 'I'm already there.'

"I stepped forward. 'You're about to get evicted.' I leapt forward, brandishing the knife. I heard it cutting through the crab shell hide. I felt the Silencer's surprise. He tried to tighten his grip on my brain. I swung the knife again and watched in delight as the monster began to bleed from the stomach. I felt the pain racing through its freakish body. I stabbed at it and smiled when I saw the blade completely disappear into its side. The creature fell to its crab knees. I extracted the knife and buried it into its upside-down head. My brain slowly relaxed as the vibration ceased. The huge half-crab half-man fell to the ground.

"Exhausted, I turned my attention to the skinner dead. They were gone, and they had taken Valerie with them. I was relieved to not have to fight again. I waited for the others to find me, but they never came. I sat down against a large tree and passed out.

***

"Covered in Silencer blood, I emerged from the woods early the next morning. Wes spotted me first and ran to help me stay on my feet. He examined my clothes and shook his head.

"'There goes the truce,' he said.

"Lou stuck her head out from behind the abandoned U-haul truck. She looked as surprised to see me as I was surprised to actually still be alive. She grabbed a bottled water and brought it to me as Wes gently helped me sit down in the back of the Escalade.

"'Valerie?' she asked.

"I took a drink and shook my head.

"Wes grumbled and threw a fist into the side of the Escalade. 'Damn it! We should have killed that thing when we had a chance!'

"'So this is my fault?' Lou asked defensively.

"Tyrone approached. 'Where is she?'

"I couldn't look him in the eyes. 'She's gone.'

"'Where is she?' he screamed

"I looked up and saw April and Little Bobby nervously standing on the shoulder of the road. They both smiled, clearly relieved I was back.

"'Tell me!' Tyrone continued to scream.

"Wes put his hand on Tyrone's shoulder. 'Hold on, kid. Keep it together.'

"Tyrone shook his hand off. 'I want to know where she is!'

"I worked up the courage and stared him in the eyes. 'No you don't.'

"He understood and collapsed to the pavement. Wes knelt down beside him and put his hand back on Tyrone's shoulder. This time Tyrone grabbed and squeezed tightly.

"Tears welled up in Lou's eyes. 'What did I do?'

ELEVEN

"The trouble that Wes had anticipated delayed our trip by two days. We spent a day in shocked silence. We all loved Valerie, even those of us who only knew her for a very short time.

"Tyrone lay on the pavement where he first fell for a full twelve hours before he moved. Wes followed him as he walked to the Honda Element he had previously used as a watchtower. He opened the door and pulled out Valerie's backpack. He hugged it to his body and stood motionless. A cool breeze picked up. We all watched him like he was a stick of dynamite that would explode at any minute. All of us except Lou, she had locked herself in an Oldsmobile Cutlas Supreme. She blamed herself for Valerie's death and it was apparent the rest of us did, too. I wasn't sure how fair it was, but we couldn't help ourselves. None of us would say it to her face, but we all felt it. I knew that without even speaking to the others.

"By mid-afternoon the next day, I decided she had been allowed to stew in her own juices long enough. It was time one of us made an attempt to alleviate her guilt. I knocked on the driver's side window of the Oldsmobile. She sat with her arms folded over her chest and shot me a devil's stare. She then resumed staring at nothing. I knocked again.

"'We have to talk,' I said.

"She didn't acknowledge me.

"'This isn't getting us anywhere. I think it's time we move on...,' I winced. I didn't mean that the way it sounded. 'I mean we should get going... to Saluda like we planned.'

"She remained silent.

"I placed my hands on the roof of the car and tapped my fingers. 'Look, Lou... soldiers die in wars. That's just the way things are.'

"'She was a kid,' Lou said.

"I ducked my head. 'True, but so are you. I'm almost a kid myself. We're going to make mistakes.'

"I felt someone tapping me on the shoulder. Startled, I twirled and fell against the car.

"Little Bobby giggled at my reaction.

"'Don't sneak up on people like that, Bobby,' I said as my heart thumped frantically.

"'Sorry,' he said. 'I just wanted to know when we're having dinner. I'm hungry.'

"I sighed and ran my fingers through my hair. 'Have whatever you want, Bobby. I don't think anyone else feels like eating.'

"Bobby shrugged and peered through the glass at Lou. 'You hungry, Miss Lou? We're supposed to have noodles tonight. Remember?'

"She turned with a confused expression. 'What are you talking about?'

"'After Valerie dies we always have noodles,' he said.

"She looked at me waiting for me to interpret for Little Bobby.

"'What do you mean we always have noodles?' I asked turning Bobby toward me.

"'I don't know,' he said. 'I'm hungry.' He walked away. 'I'll get the noodles.'

"The car door opened and Lou stepped out. 'Bobby,' she yelled. He stopped and turned to her. 'This has happened before?'

"'It happens every time I read this comic book.'

"I furrowed my brow as he walked away. It was crazy talk by a retarded kid who pretended to be the world's greatest jockey, nothing more. The expression on Lou's face told a different story. She understood exactly what Bobby was talking about.

***

"Lou paced, chewing on her fingernails. She was deep in thought. I watched her from a distance at first, afraid to interrupt the plan that she appeared to be mulling over in her head. Wes joined me.

"'She getting better?' Wes asked.

"'She's starting to snap out of it,' I said.

"Wes nodded. 'Good,' he said, sounding as if he was trying to convince himself. 'That's good. It was a mistake. A dumb mistake, but she can't let that eat her up. No, that's good. That's real good.' I could tell he didn't completely forgive Lou for what happened, but I imagine he blamed himself, too. He was the oldest of the group. He probably felt he could have overridden Lou's decision, but he let her lead. It was going to be interesting to see what happened when the next life-and-death decision had to be made. Would he let her lead again? He probably would. You don't let people lead. It just happens. Lou was a natural born leader. Wes wasn't, and he knew it. Wes cleared his throat and rubbed his hands together. 'What did you say to her to get her to come around?'

"I shrugged. 'I didn't say anything. It was Little Bobby.'

"'Bobby?' Wes said. We both turned to watch Little

Bobby sifting through the supplies. 'What did he say?'

"'Said he wanted to eat noodles for dinner.' I looked at Wes to see if that meant anything to him.

"'Yeah, so?'

"'So,' I said. 'It seems we always eat noodles after Valerie dies.'

"'What in the world is that supposed to mean?'

"'I'm not exactly sure. Something about a comic book.'

"Wes's eyes bulged. He looked as though he'd stopped breathing. After several seconds, he spoke, but couldn't manage to say anything but a series of 'Ummms' and 'Ahhhs.'

"'I take it that means something to you, too," I said.

"He nodded. 'We're back in the comic book,' he said.

"I shook my head. 'Not getting it, chief. Back in the comic book, what does that mean?'

"He smiled. 'It means there is still a way to win this thing. We're in the comic book again!' He yelled.

"'I don't think we ever left,' Lou said. She had approached unnoticed and it startled both Wes and me.

"'Somebody want to tell me what's going on?' I asked.

"'The Takers,' Lou said. 'That was a comic book that was written by Stevie Dayton, the first Storyteller. He basically wrote about everything that happened to us before it happened to us.'

"'The Délons,' Wes said. 'There ain't never been a comic book there.'

"'Not that we know of,' Lou said, 'but they're looking for the Source. What's to say the Source isn't a comic book?'

"Wes nodded. 'Could be.'

"I listened to them talk and mulled over the implications of what they were saying. I wasn't the best student in school, but I paid attention to what the pretty girls liked. I had a crush on a girl by the name of Carlie Lee in seventh grade. Her old man was a philosophy teacher at Alabama. She was Asian so I spent six weeks studying Chinese philosophers to impress her. It didn't do me a bit of good, because she was more interested in Alan Crump, the starting quarterback for our middle school's team. But I can't help but think that crush on Carlie Lee prepared me for this moment. The moment where Lou and Wes discussed the possibility that there was a comic book out there that described everything we were going to do before we did it.

"It sparked the one philosophy that challenged me, that actually made me think. A Chinese philosopher by the name of Zhuangzi once had a dream that he was a butterfly, but when he woke up he wasn't sure if he was a man dreaming he was a butterfly or a butterfly dreaming he was a man.

"Were we looking for a comic book about us or were we just characters in the comic book, living out the story as it's written?

"My head spun slightly as I tried to hold onto the thought. I shuddered and shook my head.

"'You okay?' Wes asked.

"'Fine,' I said. 'Got a chill that's all.' I stood and started to walk away.

"'I'm going to cook some noodles.' I joined Bobby and helped him search through the supplies. I wanted to ask him if we were real. If we had lived the lives we thought we had or if that was just back story for the way we behaved on the pages of the comic book. But I was sure he would just shrug his shoulders and tell me two plus two was penguin.

"We searched and searched and searched, but we came up empty. I squatted and went through a backpack I had

159

gone through three times before. Pulling out the same box of instant rice I had pulled out on all three occasions, I said, 'There ain't any noodles to be found anywhere, Little Bobby.'

"He looked dumbfounded.

"'I don't get it,' I said. 'If you've read this comic book shouldn't you know where the noodles are?'

"'I know where they are,' he said.

"I laughed. 'Sure.'

"'Tyrone's got them.'

"I leaned backwards and allowed myself to gently flop to the cold pavement. 'Then what are we doing looking through all this stuff?'

"''Cause that's what we're supposed to do.'

"'Uh-huh,' I said. 'Because that's what we do in the comic book, right?'

"He nodded.

"I held up the box of rice and shook it. 'I think you're going to have to settle for rice...'

"'You looking for this?' Tyrone said, holding out a family sized bag of Ramen noodles.

"I slowly reached out and took it from him. 'Yeah, where...?'

"'It was in Valerie's backpack with this,' he said handing me a folded piece of paper.

"I unfolded it and read the note inside. 'For Bobby. Give to Archie.'

"Bobby took the bag of noodles out of my hand, 'Told you.'

"'She knew?' I asked Bobby.

"He nodded with a hangdog look on his face. 'She's nice. I don't like this part of the story. I didn't want the monster to get her this time, but... no matter how many times I tell her it still happens. Don't be mad.'

"I stood. 'Mad? You should have told her. You should tell all of us what is going to happen.'

"He handed the noodles back to me. 'April cooks.'

"April walked up on cue. 'I'm hungry. When are we going to eat?' She spotted the bag of Ramen noodles in my hand.

'Sweet.' She took the noodles out of my hand. 'I can cook the crap out of some Ramen noodles. I lived off these things my last semester.' She disappeared behind the truck we were standing in front of to start preparing the noodles. I watched the whole thing play out with wonder.

"'Tyrone will leave to help her,' Bobby said.

"Confused, Tyrone looked at Bobby and then me. 'What's going on?'

"'I'll explain later,' I said. 'Go help April.'

"'You have to say please,' Bobby said.

"'Please,' I said.

"Clearly still confused, Tyrone decided to do as I requested.

"'What happens now?' I asked.

"'You ask me what happens,' he said.

"'Besides that?'

"Lou and Wes joined us.

"'Now they ask me,' Bobby said.

"Lou said, 'I think it's time you tell us what you know, Bobby.'

"'See.'

"'Okay,' I said. 'This isn't getting us anywhere.' I urged Lou and Wes to let me handle the interrogation. 'Bobby, do you know what the Source is.'

"He laughed. 'You never like my answer,' he said.

"'Try me,' I sighed.

"'Yes.'

"There was a long moment of silence as I waited for

him to follow up with more information, but he never did. 'What is it?' I shouted.

"'I can't say. I'm not really supposed to be telling you anything.'

"'But you told Valerie.'

"'And it didn't help.'

"'So, you still told her.'

"He dropped his chin to his chest. 'I get in trouble every time I go back. Dr. Bashir gets really mad.'

"'Bashir?' Lou said.

"Bobby nodded slowly. Whispering, he said, 'He doesn't want you to win.'

"'Is he listening?' Wes asked.

"Bobby shook his head. 'He's reading.'

"We all stood frozen in time. I searched the sky for a giant pair of eyes staring down at us. Violet clouds glided above our heads, but there was no evidence of pupils scanning unseen words in the ether that surrounded us.

"I reflexively grabbed Bobby's hand and squeezed. 'Are we real?'

"His face grimaced in pain. 'What do you mean?' he asked yanking his hand away.

"I pulled back. 'I mean do we exist, or are we just characters in a comic book?'

"Wes snickered. 'Well, I can tell you for damn sure that I'm real. I got a family... had a family, sister, her husband and what not. I'm real as this old beat up truck,' he said patting the tailgate.'

"Lou fixated on the tailgate. 'What if the truck's not real?'

"Wes rolled his eyes. 'Good God almighty! Don't tell me you're going to start up on this, too. It's nonsense, Lou. Crazy as crazy can be.'

"'Crazy,' I said. I spun the word around in my head.

'He doesn't like that word.'

"'Who doesn't?' Wes asked.

"I thought about the question. 'I don't know.' I mouthed the word a few times. Then whispered, 'Crazy. Crazy. Crazy. Who doesn't like that word?' A vision flashed in my head. I had no face. I reached up and touched my nose. The vision was gone. To Bobby, 'Do you know?'

"He shook his head. He looked frightened. 'This part's not in the comic book.'

"I suddenly felt woozy and doubled over placing my hands on my knees. 'Something's changed.'

"Wes placed a meaty hand on my back. 'I think that Silencer got inside that head of yours and rattled some things around.'

"A scream shot through the sky. We all took off to investigate. When we rounded the other side of the truck, we saw Lou with a pot in her hand standing over a flattened and crumbled mound of Ramen noodles. Tyrone stood next to her panting.

"'What happened?' Lou asked.

"'Tyrone just knocked the noodles out of my hand and started stomping on them.'

"Tyrone didn't defend himself. He held out a piece of paper. 'I found this in Valerie's backpack just now.'

"Lou took the paper out of his hand. 'It's a note.' She read it out loud. 'Don't eat the noodles.' She looked up. Her brow was furrowed. 'It's signed by someone named Millie B. Story.'

Oz

SEVEN

Millie B. Story.

I look at the words written on the notebook. She had now made it into Scoop-face's session. Who is Millie B. Story? I remain in the janitor's closet writing the name over and over again. Light creeping in through the bottom of the door illuminates the room. I see the shadows of people's feet passing the closet as they travel through the hall. I am sure I will be discovered at any moment, but I don't care. I am now consumed with figuring out who Millie B. Story is, and what she wants with me. From Scoop-face's story, I have determined that she is here to help.

A light tapping comes at the door. "Boss," Bones whispers. I continue writing Millie B. Story's name. I don't answer. "We gotta go." He waits for my reply, but it doesn't come.

"Boss?"

The door slowly pushes open, and Bones slips in. "Oz?"

"Down here," I say from my hiding spot in the corner of the closet.

He sighs heavily. "Thank goodness. I thought you went without me."

My left eyebrow shoots up. "Went where without you?"

His face contorts and twists as he realizes he's said something he shouldn't have. "You know, back to your room. Archie would have my head if I let you go back unescorted."

"You're a bad liar," I say. "That's good to know." I stand. "Who's Millie B. Story?"

"I don't know."

I shove him. "Tell me." I fight to keep my voice down.

"I don't know. I swear."

"I told you, you're a bad liar, Bones."

He looks down and nervously tugs on his pant leg.

"We're getting nowhere, and I'm tired of this damn closet," I say. "Tell me who Millie B. Story is." He starts mumbling something under his breath. I can't make out what he's saying. I lean in, "What?"

He speaks more clearly and raises his voice to just above a whisper. "Snarkel, snapper, momma, jaws, spot, jumper, hambone, Charlie boy."

"Stop talking nonsense!" I say much too loudly.

"Snarkel, snapper, momma, jaws, spot, jumper, hambone, Charlie boy," he repeats.

I shake him by the shoulders. "Bones don't do this to me. I need to know."

I hear a clicking on the linoleum floor of the hallway outside the closet. Feet... claws... nails tapping against the cold hard foundation of the world outside our small room.

"Snarkel, snapper, momma, jaws, spot, jumper, hambone, Charlie boy," Bones says again. His eyes roll back in his head and a toothy grin protrudes from his skull-like face. A series of growls rumbles through the heavy closet door. I can hear the clacking of teeth as jaws snap shut.

"What are you doing?" I ask Bones. My mouth is dry and my palms begin to sweat.

"Calling in for back-up," he says.

A scratching comes at the door. The growls grow more intense. "You're supposed to be helping me," I say.

He grabs the handle of the door without looking and slowly pulls the door open. "This is helping."

"Wait, wait, wait," I say panicked.

A large animal leaps through the open doorway and knocks me to the ground with a violent thud. Another animal follows and another and another. I hear wild barking. A saliva drenched tongue covers my face. More than one, three, four, too many to count. I push myself back across the floor. A dog whines. It takes me several seconds to determine that these mad dogs weren't attacking me. They weren't mad at all. They are ecstatic.

"Dogs?" I say.

"Snarkel, snapper, momma, jaws, spot, jumper, hambone, Charlie boy," Bones says. His pupils back front and center.

I count the wagging tails. "Eight dogs."

Bones smiles.

"Wes's Taker Killers." I pat one of the mutts. "This is what happened to them."

Bones introduces me to each one, and gives his reasoning for their names. Snarkel makes a snarkel noise when he sneezes. Snapper snaps at the others for no reason. Jaws has an impressive set of choppers. Spot has a single white spec of fur on her snout. Jumper leaps like a kangaroo. Hambone can fit five large hambones in his mouth and Charlie Boy is his favorite.

"Named him after me," Bones says. "Used to call him Charlie's Boy, but he ain't nobody's boy. He's the leader. Alpha male, I guess is what you call him. He's just Charlie Boy now."

I smile. "They look good, Bone... Charlie."

"Thanks," he grins. "They have been itching to get to this thing. It's been tough holding them back."

"Where?"

He thinks about the question. "I don't really know. They's good hiders. When I need them, they come a running. They're just about the greatest dogs that ever lived." Snarkel jumps up and puts his big paws on Charlie's bony chest.

"Nobody else knows about them?"

"Nobody but Archie. He put me in charge of them when he come here." He scratches behind Snarkel's ears.

I poke my head outside the closet door. It's empty. Back to Bones, "You need to hide them..." I stand in silent wonder. The dogs are gone. "Where?..."

"I told you," Bones smiles. "They's good hiders."

"C'mon," I say. I step into the hallway and quickly head down the corridor.

"Where we going?" Bones asks as he struggles to keep up with my pace.

"You're going to escort me to Archie's room."

***

"You're not telling me everything," I say to Scoop-face.

He sits on the edge of his bed. The missing parts of his face do not disgust me as much as they had before. I can see the young man he used to be in the way he sat. His broad shoulders are perfectly aligned and his posture is proud and straight. For the moment, he is not Scoop-face. He is Archie. He smiles. "I don't know everything."

I shake my head. "You know what I mean. You're not telling me everything you know."

He hesitates. "Are you a butterfly, Oz?"

I think about the question and remember the story of the Chinese philosopher from his session. "No, Archie. I'm not a butterfly. I am a man... or a boy..."

"Creyshaw," Scoop-face said. "You are a creyshaw."

I nod. "Okay, I am a creyshaw."

"Or are you?" he asks.

I cover my eyes with the palms of my hands and bend back, fighting the urge to scream. "What are you doing to me?"

"Are you a creyshaw dreaming you're a man in a psychiatric ward in the year 2033 or are you a man in a psychiatric ward dreaming you're a creyshaw in the year 2008?"

I drop my hands to my sides. "I don't know. I don't know. I don't know. That's why I'm here. You tell me."

"I can't," he said. "You've got to figure that out on your own." He places his hand on the bedpost and lifts himself to his feet.

"What are you?" I ask.

He smiles. "I'm a man without a face trying to make up for all the mistakes I've made in my life."

"Your family?"

His smile quickly disappears. "Among others." He says as he clumsily steps forward. He whispers. "She changed the story."

I stroke my chin and whisper back, "Millie B. Story?"

He nods. "She's confused them."

"Them who?"

He signals for Bones to enter from the doorway. "We've never made it this far. This is the longest you've remembered. You gave her time to change the story. We are one step away." He grabs Bones' elbow. "Take me to the cafeteria. I'm in the mood for some soup." To me, "What is Lou's real name?"

I run my fingers through my hair. "I can't remember."

"You will," he says. "Let's go, Charlie." They stop at the open doorway and Archie says, "Do you have a notebook?"

I pull the small notebook from the janitor's closet out of my back pocket. "Yeah."

"Do me a favor," he says. "Write down 'Lou's real name' on the last page with writing on it."

I snicker. "I think I can remember that."

"Indulge me," he says. "Do an old faceless man a favor."

I pause. He is up to something. I turn to the page where I had scribbled Millie B. Story's name down several times and write down "Lou's real name."

He grins. "That-a-boy." He squeezes Bones' elbow and they disappear down the hallway.

I stare at the empty doorway for several seconds. He was a strange man. But then again, he was in a loony bin. I glance down at that notebook. Right under Millie B. Story's name are the words "Lou's real name." I look back up at the vacant entryway. Could it be?

***

Lou's name is not Millie B. Story. I am sure of that. I lay in my bed churning Millie B. Story's name over in my mind's eye. I chastise myself several times for not being able to remember Lou's real name. She told me. I can't remember where or when, but I can picture the expression of her face when she said it.

I sit up in bed. The decaying face of a woman looks at me from the foot of the bed. "Are you Millie B. Story?" I ask her. She stares at me blankly, as the dead are apt to do. "I guess not. I don't even think Millie B. Story is Millie B.

Story," I laugh. The dead woman does not join in. I yawn.

Nurse Kline's face appears in the square window of my room and the dead scatter. I wave to her not expecting her to wave back, but she does. She looks different somehow. Expectant almost. She's not merely checking in on me as she normally does. I catch a glimpse of my hand as I finish my wave. It looks different, too. Some of the hair is gone. I'm too afraid to let myself think it, but my hand looks younger.

A dead boy whispers from the corner of the room, "I don't even think Millie B. Story is Millie B. Story."

"Copycat," I say. I see the notebook on the floor by the bed and pick it up. I begin to doodle. "Millie isn't Millie," I say in a sing-song tone. A few of the dead join in. We form an eerie chorus that begins to chill me to the bone. "That's enough," I say, but they continue without me. The boy who had spoken earlier repeats his line, "I don't even think Millie B. Story is Millie B. Story." I cup my hands over my ears. "Shut up!" I scream. I peer down at the notebook now resting in my lap. It hits me. "Millie B. Story isn't Millie B. Story. Millie B. Story is Lou's real name." I smile. "Not her real name, no. But her real name is in Millie B. Story." I had been looking at it all wrong. It's not the name that matters. It's the letters in the name. I frantically start rearranging them in the notebook. I am terrible at these kinds of puzzles. I rearrange and rearrange and rearrange until I have a jumbled mess of letters on the page in front of me.

The door to my room opens and I shove the notebook under my pillow. Chester walks in. "Doc Graham wants to see you," he says.

"What for?" I ask.

"Don't know," he says, "Does it matter?"

"Not to you," I say.

He snaps his fingers. "Now you're getting it." He steps aside and sticks out his meaty paw, inviting me to pass through the open door. "After you, Nutty McCrazy."

I hesitate. I am reluctant to leave my notebook behind. It's as if the words will vanish from the page if I leave my room. Chester clamps down on my shoulder with his thick, heavy fingers and pushes me toward the door.

"Apparently you have this idea that I'm a patient man," Chester groans. "I'm not."

I flinch in pain. We head down the hallway toward Dr. Graham's office. "Hey, Chester," I say. "You ever wonder if you're a man dreaming you're a butterfly or a butterfly dreaming you're a man."

"What?" He says in a dubious tone.

"Are you a butterfly or a man?"

"You see wings on my back?"

I scoff because he doesn't understand the question. "The way I see it," I say, "butterflies don't have much of a brain. They might not even know the difference between a dream and reality."

"So?"

"So, I know the difference. I can't be a dream."

"Don't know what you're talking about, but if you got a butterfly brain you probably ain't spending a whole lot of time on what's real and what's not." We turned the corridor. "Besides, butterflies don't sleep. How can they dream?"

***

The first question I ask Dr. Graham is if butterflies sleep. He is of course confused. I don't pursue the line of questioning. He sits across from me writing in his notebook. We sit for a full five minutes before he speaks.

"How have you been enjoying your GP pass?"

"Fine," I say.

"Making friends?"

"A few."

"I hear you've been seen with Archie Maynard."

I am tentative, "Yeah."

"What do you know about Archie?" He seems to still be focusing on his notebook. He has mastered the ability to multitask. I almost feel like I am interrupting him.

"He can't wear glasses," I say expecting to be reprimanded. He chuckles instead. "No he can't. Do you know what happened to his face?"

I shook my head. "Never came up."

"He breathed in a rare mold that infected his sinuses. The doctors removed his nose and eyes to save his life. His family abandoned him because of his deformity. His own son would scream at the sight of him."

"I thought his family... died," I say.

"He told you that?"

I shrug. "More or less."

"They are alive. His son is grown now. He calls periodically to check on him, but he's never visited. He's still traumatized by his father's appearance."

"Why are you telling me this?" I ask.

"Because I'm concerned about your recovery. Surrounding yourself with the wrong people isn't healthy," he says finally setting his notebook aside. "Archie is perfectly nice, but he's not... the most rational person. He makes up stories to help himself cope with his condition. The world has rejected him. His loved ones want nothing to do with him. He's created a fantasy world to give himself a reason to live."

"You brought me here to tell me not to hang out with crazy people in a crazy house?"

He closes his eyes and calms himself before he speaks. "You know I don't like that word." Eyes open now. "And no that's not why I brought you here. You have a visitor."

My heart almost explodes. "A visitor... is it...?"

"Millie B. Story. She is quite persistent. I'm sorry I didn't confer with you first. I suppose that's what I'm doing with you now. She showed up on the premises today unannounced. My first inclination was to send her away, but then I thought better of it." He scoots his chair closer to me. "I've decided that you should make the determination whether or not you want to see her. You've shown great strides over the past weeks. You may be ready for this."

"I-I-I..." I can feel sweat forming on my upper lip. I reach up to wipe it off and I notice my hand is trembling. I swallow and breathe in deeply. "How do we do this?" I ask. "Is there a visitor's room..." I laugh. "I don't even know if this place has a visitor's room. It seems like I should know something like that."

Dr. Graham gently pats my leg. "You've never had visitors before. It's all right. We can do this in my office."

"Here? Now?"

He responds to my shocked expression. "You don't have to do this at all, Oz."

I nod. "No, I should... I should... I definitely should."

He presses a button on his pen and Chester enters the room. "Bring Miss Story in please," the doc says.

As Chester leaves to do as directed, I feel a certain amount of disappointment. The pen is more than a pen. And what happened to the bell?

Time passes slowly as I await Chester to return with my visitor. I have no idea how I will react. Is she... could she be...

The door opens again. I clasp my hands together and

place them on my lap. I don't know what to do. I want to stand and greet her with a friendly smile, but I am afraid I will stumble to my feet and give her an off-putting sense of apprehension. So I sit.

I hear her shoes beat against the floor as she approaches. Dr. Graham stands and extends a hand. I stare at his hand waiting for hers to zoom in across my field of vision. Perhaps I will recognize it, and I will feel immediately at ease.

The hand appears and grips Dr. Graham's firmly. It is a strong hand covered by smooth ageless skin. The nails are long, but not too long, strong and healthy. The wrist is the only other exposed flesh. She is wearing a light, dignified coat.

"Miss Story," Dr. Graham says. "Have a seat." He points to a chair that Chester has placed next to his.

I still can't bring myself to look at her face. She settles into the chair and I turn away.

"Thank you for doing this," she says.

"Don't thank me," Dr. Graham says. "This was Oz's decision."

I can feel her smile. "Thank you, Oz."

I finally work up the courage to look her in the face. I am amazed. I have no reaction. I do not recognize her. I would recognize Lou. This is not her. It can't be. She is a beautiful woman. The same features and build as I imagine Lou would have if she were the age of the woman sitting in front of me, but yet, instinct tells me this is not Lou.

"Do you remember me?" she asks.

I shake my head.

"I'm afraid you have us both at a disadvantage, Miss Story," Dr. Graham says. "There is no record of a Millie B. Story in Oz's file."

"That doesn't surprise me," she says. She hesitates.

"What is your life like outside of this building, Dr. Graham?"

"Pardon me?"

"What is your family like?"

He tilts his head. "Family? I'm not sure what that has to do with Oz..."

She locks me in a stare. "It has everything to do with him."

"My family is... I have a lovely wife and... two daughters." The doc strains as he describes his family.

"A lovely wife?" Millie B. Story says. To me, "Don't you think that's an odd way to put it?"

I nod. "Yes, very odd."

"And you seem to have a hard time recalling them." She says to the doctor.

"I just find this a bit unusual," he answers.

"What's your favorite color, Dr. Graham?"

"Color?"

"Your favorite food? Your middle name? Do you have any pets? C'mon, these aren't hard questions."

"I... I..." He is panicked and his face is flush.

"Doc," Chester says. "You okay?"

He looks at the giant orderly. "I don't know."

She turns to Chester. "What about you? If I asked you the same questions, would you have any answers?"

"Don't drag me into this," Chester says. "I hate animals, and I ain't never been married."

She shrugs. "Your middle name?"

He has the same pained look as Dr. Graham.

"How about your last name?"

He strokes his chin with the palm of his brawny hand.

She turns to me. "They don't know, Oz. Don't you find that the least bit strange?"

I marvel at the terrified faces of Dr. Graham and

Chester. "What's going on?"

"They have no answers because there are no answers. This isn't real, Oz."

"Stop," Dr. Graham says.

"Not real?" I say.

"Not real. They don't know it. They think it's real. But it's just a story, created for you so the Délons can find the Source. You're the key, Oz."

"This is ridiculous," Dr. Graham shouts.

"We don't have much time," she says. "The Storytellers are adapting the story as we speak."

"I thought the Storytellers were on my side."

"They are, but the ones being held by the Délons are being forced to write this story. You're a prisoner being manipulated so you can lead them to the Source. You have to break out of this story."

"They wrote you in to help me?" I ask.

"Yes, but we don't have much time. As soon as the Délons discover what the Storytellers have done, I'll be erased from the story. Do you understand?"

I nod. "I think I do."

"It doesn't matter. Get back to the cave. You have to be there when Archie gets there."

I lean back and in a blink she disappears from the chair. She reappears in a second blink.

"They've found me," she says. "We're out of time."

"Wait," I bark. "Are you Lou?"

She smiles. "Remember my name."

Dr. Graham suddenly speaks. "My favorite color is blue."

There is a flash of bright light. I am sitting in Dr. Graham's office watching him write in his notepad. Millie B. Story is no longer there. The chair she was sitting in is gone. Chester is gone.

"Why do you want to know if butterflies sleep?" Dr. Graham asks.

I squirm in my seat. They have erased her.

***

I do not wait for Bones to escort me to the janitors closet for Scoop-face's next session. I am in the closet hours before Scoop-face is even due to arrive in the doctor's office. Bones probably fell to pieces when he didn't find me in my room. Perhaps he felt "I went without him" again.

I sit on the closet floor going over the puzzle that is Millie B. Story. I arrange the letters in every possible combination and the name still eludes me. Each time I hit a dead end, I grow more discouraged. I try closing my eyes and forcing myself to remember. A pattern flashes in my brain. A group of three letters: MIL. Another group of letters comes to me: STO. I write it down on the notebook. MIL STO. I say it out loud. "Mil Sto."

"Ready to get my hypnosis on, Doc," I hear Scoop-face's voice travel through the vent.

Dr. Graham's muffled voice answers back, "There is more to your treatment than regression therapy."

"Right," Scoop-face says, "and we can get to that next week. Today... today we get me back to Lou and the gang. Things are just about to heat up, and they need me."

"This is what I didn't want to happen," Dr. Graham responds with a heavy sigh. "This is not helping you to progress."

"Well, duh, Doc. That's because we haven't seen it through to the end."

I can picture Dr. Graham's face as he mulls over Scoop-face's logic. "This is the last session."

"I'm cool with that," Scoop-face says. I can hear the relief in his voice as he walks to the couch.

Scoop-face

THIRTEEN

"The gorillas had formed a highly organized ban. In fact it wasn't just gorillas in their group. It included every kind of primate you can think of, chimps, baboons, orangutans, macaques, you name it. They lived in a well-defined order. The smaller monkeys were on the bottom rung. They served the bigger apes, scavenged for food, assigned to grooming duties. The macaques were next up. They kept the smaller monkeys in line. The baboons were the guards. They formed a primate fence around the perimeter of the encampment. They sounded the alarm when any unexpected visitors approached (such as us). The orangutans and chimps shared the next place in the chain of command. For lack of a better description, they were the diplomats and strategists, and they policed the others to make sure everyone (or everyape) was keeping to their assigned duties.

"The gorillas were very clearly in charge. They strolled through the outdoor citadel deliberately and proudly. The other primates moved out of their way without argument. It was a wonder to see. I expected to see a horde of inner species conflicts when we first arrived. But it was as if the apes knew they served a greater purpose. That's not to say there weren't any underlying tensions among the group. There were, especially among the baboons, the colorful ones, the mandrills. They were fierce looking creatures with canines bigger than my fingers. They greeted us with a frightening charge, teeth exposed, their short tales raised. They reluctantly calmed when Ajax stepped ahead of our group and signed to them that we were brothers. Warriors looking for a sanctuary.

"A female chimp by the name of Kavi was called. The mandrill signed to her, all the while huffing and seemingly battling his inclination to call for an all out attack on us by the other baboons.

"Kavi signed back and apparently reprimanded the mandrill for what must have been his suggestion for a hostile resolution to what to do with the new visitors. The chimp knuckle walked to Ajax and sat in front of him. She signed something.

"'What's going on?' I asked Lou.

"'She asked Ajax his name.'

"Ajax signed back and the chimp bowed her head. "'Is that good?' I asked.

"Wes smiled. 'Very good. Ajax is kind of a rock star among apes. Everyone knows him.'

"'Nice,' I said. I turned to April and Little Bobby and gave them the thumbs up. I heard the rustling of the trees beside me seconds before I was knocked to the ground. A large mandrill sat on my chest and peered down at me. It's mouth in a toothy grimace.

"'Archie!' Little Bobby screamed.

"Ajax roared forth and knocked the mandrill off of me. The two apes momentarily squared off before the smaller baboon thought better of it. It backed away and eventually bowed its head.

"Wes helped me up. 'What did you do?'

"'Nothing,' I said. 'I just gave April and Bobby the thumbs up so they wouldn't be scared.'

"'Yeah, well I think it backfired on you. We all just

about pissed ourselves,' Wes said. 'I suggest you not do that again.'

"'Way ahead of you, pal.'

"Kavi guided us through the winding pathway to a clearing filled with hundreds of apes. We were at about 2,200 feet elevation. It made for chilly temperatures and the apes were all huddled together to give each other warmth. There was the remnants of an old cabin on the outskirts of the clearing. A picnic table or two was tucked away throughout the area positioned under towering hemlock trees.

"A large silverback approached. The gorilla was bigger than Ajax by at least fifty pounds. It surveyed our group with a stern, almost angry expression. Kavi signed to him. The silverback's eyes widened, and it too bowed its enormous head to Ajax. The other apes all gathered around in a semi-circle and hooted and screeched. It was a celebration like I had never seen before. It was as if they had been waiting for Ajax.

"The big silverback's name was Ariabod. He was the leader, and he ruled with an iron fist. I witnessed him charge other apes who didn't give us adequate space, and even tackle a particularly curious orangutan to the ground. The orange, spindly-armed ape screamed bloody murder and hobbled off after Ariabod let him up.

"Ajax and Ariabod sat among a small group of chimps and blackback gorillas. They carried on a remarkable conversation using American Sign language, punctuated by the occasional grunt or screech. The humans weren't allowed to participate in the conversation. Lou sat on a picnic table with Kimball lying at her feet. I joined her.

"'I don't get it,' I said. 'How do they all know how to do that? Sign language, I mean.'

"Lou kept her eyes on the chatty group of apes. 'Don't

know. Not much use in trying to make sense of anything that goes on in this world. If you ask Ajax, he'll tell ya' they always knew how to do it. They just didn't have any use for it until now.'

"'You know what they're talking about?'

"She narrowed her eyes and crinkled her nose. 'I can pick up a word every now and then. Ajax is trying to find out where the cave is. Kavi said she knows of a cave. Ariabod is begging Ajax for his help.'

"'What kind of help?'

"'I can't figure it out. Something's coming.'

"I cringed at the thought. 'Something like what?'

"'Don't know. Whatever it is has the big silverback pretty nervous.' She leaned toward the group even though it served no real purpose. It wouldn't help her 'hear' the sign language any better.

"'What about the Keeper? Any word on that?'

"She nodded. 'Ariabod knows where to find the Keeper. He's trying to make a deal. He'll take us to the cave and the Keeper if we'll help him with whatever is coming.'

"'Of course,' I said sarcastically. 'It can't just be easy.' I sat on the picnic table next to her. 'So this something... this means we're in for a fight, right?'

"'It usually does,' She said.

"Wes joined us. 'What do you reckon has got that Ariabod all shook up?'

"'Maybe it's Bashir or Délons or Silencers,' I said. 'Pick your poison.'

'Nah,' Wes replied. 'These monkeys can hold their own with the likes of them. They don't need us for that.'

"'Then Dacs maybe,' I said.

"Wes and I talked and paid little attention to Lou. She stood and drifted closer to the group of apes without us noticing. We talked about the coming fight and the possible make-up of our as of yet unknown enemy.

"'Humans,' Lou said so softly we barely heard her.

"Wes and I were surprised she was no longer sitting at the table.

"'You say something, sweetie?' Wes asked.

"'Humans,' she said still staring at the apes as they signed. 'It's humans.'

"'Humans,' Wes said. 'Like us?'

"She turned back to Wes and me. 'Not like us.'

"'Carl,' I said.

***

"I left Wes and Lou once we had confirmed that it was Carl and his soldiers headed our way. A pair of spider monkeys had spotted them about a day behind us. They had been following us almost from the beginning. I tried to tell myself it was a bad thing, but the truth was I was glad. I owed Carl for what happened to Tank, and I was going to enjoy making him pay.

"As I plotted my revenge, Bobby snuck up behind me. 'You going to hurt Mr. Carl?'

"I jumped at the sound of his voice. I placed my hand on my chest to feel my thumping heart. 'I hope so, Bobby.'

"'It's not right, you know.'

"'What's not right?'

"'Hurting somebody. My momma said God wants us to love each other. Even our enemies.'

"'No offense, Bobby, but things have changed. There's a whole new set of rules we gotta live by, and new rule number one is I get to hurt Mr. Carl for what he did to Tank.'

"'I don't think that's right, I mean about the new rules

and all. It's the same rules...'

"'Bobby!' I shouted. 'Go away."

"He shook his head. 'I can't. I gotta tell you about what's in you.'

"I shivered at the statement. I imagined a sundry of different creatures crawling underneath my flesh. 'Wha... What do you mean?'

"'In the book, I was supposed to tell you after we had the noodles, only we never had the noodles cause Tyrone smashed them on a count he got that note from that lady. So, I forgot, but I figure if I tell you maybe the story will be back the way it's supposed to be.'

"'What's in me, Bobby?'

"He motioned for me to lean in closer so I did. 'Magic,' he whispered.

"'Magic?' I said. 'You mean I have magical powers, like a wizard or warlock or something?'

"Bobby smiled. 'That would be really cool,' he said excitedly. 'Do you know any magic tricks?'

"I shook my head in frustration. 'Whoa, wait, step back. You just said that there is magic in me. What kind of magic?'

"Bobby rolled his eyes back as if he were literally searching his brain for the answer. 'I don't know. I think I used to know, but the story changed and I don't remember some things too good. All I know is the magic will go away if you hurt Mr. Carl.'

"'What good is magic if I can't use it to hurt the one guy who deserves it?'

"Little Bobby shrugged. 'I didn't know magic was supposed to hurt people. I seen a guy saw a lady in half before, but he put her back together so that's okay.'

"'Gee, thanks,' I said. 'This has been real helpful. You got any other useless crap to tell me. Maybe you want to tell my I'm part elf and Easter bunny, too.'

"Completely missing my sarcasm, Bobby shook his head. 'Nope, I never heard that before. Just the magic thing. It's supposed to help you.'

"'Oh, yeah, you've been a huge help, Bobby.'

"Again, my sarcasm went over his head. 'Thanks,' he said walking away. I watched him in disbelief. I couldn't wait to hand him over to his Keeper. He passed Lou as she approached.

"'He's right, you know,' she said

"'Right about what? He didn't say anything.'

"She stood in front of me with her hands in her back pockets. She kicked at the ground as she talked. She looked her age again. '"Yes he did,' she said. 'You just didn't listen.'

"'Telling me that there is magic in me doesn't do me a bit of good. Telling me I can shoot death rays out of my eyes, or bench press 10,000 pounds, now that's helpful.'

"'You were chosen to be a creyshaw for a reason. There's something in you that makes you worthy.'

"I waved her off. 'Please, I drew the short straw that's all. If I have anything in me, it's a vein of bad luck a 100 miles wide. I'm magically unlucky.'

"She shook her head. 'You're wrong. I can see a lot of the same qualities in you that I saw in Oz.' She paused after his name came out of her mouth. It pained her to hear the words. She Shook off the urge to cry and breathed in deeply. 'Whatever. It doesn't really matter what you think. It will all work out.'

"Kavi slowly loomed in from the brush behind Lou. The chimp positioned itself between us and scratched her hairy shoulder while she deliberately avoided eye contact with us.

"'She want something?' I asked.

"'She's here to take you to your Keeper,' Lou said.

"'Keeper? What now?'

"'It's your first priority.'

"I couldn't believe what I was hearing. 'Oh, no, no, no. I'm not going anywhere. We made a deal with Ariabod.'

"'And we are going to keep that deal. You aren't. Kavi knows where to find your Keeper. You'll take Bobby to him.'

"'Maybe you didn't hear me. I said no.'

"She stepped forward, a steely look in her eyes. 'I'm sorry,' she said, 'I didn't mean to give you the impression that you had a choice.'

"'Don't play tough with me, Lou...'

"'I'm not playing,' she said. 'You don't seem to understand the gravity of the situation we're in. You think the world ended and our only mission is to survive. Well, you're dead wrong. Our mission is to do more than survive. Our mission is to make up for all the things that got us here. Your first step in doing that is getting Little Bobby to his Keeper.'

"I grit my teeth. A vision of Tank shuttered in my head. He was tied to the post. The lung locusts flew in and covered him from head to toe. He choked and struggled to breath. 'He killed Tank,' I said.

"'And he'll pay,' she said. 'I'll make sure of it. I promise.' Kavi signed. She repeated the same gestures several times while Lou studied them.

"'What is she saying?' I asked.

"Lou squinted and then smiled. 'You don't want to know.'

"'Yeah, I think I do,' I said.

"'She thinks you're cute.

"I almost gasped. 'Oh... ewww...' I looked at Kavi. 'No offense, but... ewww.'

"'Relax,' Lou said. 'She's not in love with you. Cute can also mean stupid but in a harmless way. She says you have always been her favorite.'

"'What is that supposed to mean?'

"'The apes,' Lou said. 'They've always known about this. They have passed these stories down about this time, about us, about the creyshaw, the Destroyers, the Keepers, the Storytellers. It is apart of their folklore.'

"I shook my head. 'That makes no sense on so many levels. First of all, apes can't talk... well, not in the real world, the one where we come from.'

"'Just because we can't hear them doesn't mean they can't talk,' Lou said.

"'Okay, then,' I said. 'You tell me how they can know things that haven't happened yet.'

"She smiled. 'As soon as you explain to me why there are guys running around with purple skin and spiders growing out of their head, or how dead people eaten by bugs can get up and walk around or why the sky is purple...'

"'All right,' I said holding up my hand. 'That's enough. I get it.' I looked at Kavi. 'Why am I her favorite?'

"'I don't know,' Lou said. 'I'll ask.' With that, Lou clumsily worked through a series of signs.

"Kavi smiled and effortlessly signed back.

"Lou looked mildly stunned by Kavi's answer. She seemed almost too embarrassed to tell me. 'She... She says it is because of the way you love your son.'

"I stumbled back. 'My son... she knows?'

"Lou nodded. 'She says you keep him in your heart and that is what makes you a great warrior. You have two hearts.'

"I dropped to a knee. The guilt was consuming me. 'I betrayed my son,' I said quietly. 'She's wrong about me.'

"Lou cleared her throat. 'Maybe the magic little Bobby sees in you is your son.'

"My stomach rumbled and turned. I felt as though I could vomit at any moment. 'You're not playing fair, you know.'

"'I know.'

"I groan, mad because I don't have a choice. 'All right. You win. I'll take Bobby to his Keeper.'

"Lou smiled. 'You're doing the right thing.'

"'Yeah, yeah, whatever. So it's me, Bobby, and Kavi.'

"'And Anuenue.'

"The colorful mandrill that had attacked me earlier emerged from the trees behind Lou. It formed a comical grin and bared it's imposing teeth.'

"'Let me guess,' I said. 'Anuenue.'

***

"April begged to join Bobby and me, but I convinced her that she would be safer with the others. We were headed into a situation we didn't know anything about. At least here, with the others, she knew what was coming, and she had an army to back her up. The more I spoke with her the more I wished I was staying, too.

"Anuenue lead our small caravan followed by Kavi and little Bobby. I brought up the rear. As we headed deeper into the woods, I must have looked over my shoulder a hundred times. I wondered if the battle had started yet, if April was all right, if Lou had gotten back her sword yet. The farther we got from them the more I felt I needed to be with them.

"Little Bobby began to regale us with his unique rendition of 'I've Got Friends In Low Places.' Anuenue howled in protest after about the seventh straight verse. I sensed the baboon was about to carry his frustration to a new level at any moment, so I decided I better find a way to distract little Bobby and get him off the song.

"'Yo, Bobby tell me about how you came up with the Bashir.'

"'Huh?' Bobby said.

"'The Bashir, how did you come up with them?'

"'I didn't come up with the Bashir.'

"'What?'

"'No, that was Adwin,' Bobby said.

"I stopped and turned him by his shoulder. 'Wait a minute... Wait a minute... You're not the Bashir Storyteller.'

"He shook his head. 'No, my friend is... Adwin.'

"'I don't understand. Lou said you were a Storyteller.'

"'I am. I'm just not the Bashir Storyteller. Adwin is and he's in Délon City... in jail or something. I'm not really sure what they do with us when they capture us.'

"By now Anuenue and Kavi figured out we had stopped so they backtracked to join us. Anuenue barked and displayed his huge fangs to try and intimidate us into moving. Kavi signed something of which I couldn't even begin to understand. They didn't like the fact that we had stopped. That much I understood.

"I stuck my hand out, palm down and motioned for them stay calm. 'We'll go in a second.' To Bobby, 'If you're not the Bashir Storyteller, which Storyteller are you?'

"'They are called Myrmidons,' I heard a voice say. A horse trotted out from behind a thicket of trees with a single Délon on its back. His spider leg hair do was in tightly woven cornrows. His deadeyes beamed from their purple sockets. Behind him I could see dozens more Délons standing in neat military formation.

"I looked at Kavi. 'I guess this is what you were trying to tell me.'

"She nodded with a disgusted look on her face.

"The Délon dismounted. 'General Roy,' he said.

"I stepped in front of Bobby.

"'These are my soldiers,' he said motioning to the men who were not so cleverly concealed. He sniffed the air. 'And you are this Storytellers warrior, I presume.'

"I looked to Kavi for direction but she had nothing to offer and considering my inability to read sign langue, no way to communicate it to me.

"'I am creyshaw,' I said.

"General Roy smiled and the sight of it sent pin pricks up my spine. 'I see you've taken to the Silencer's word. Fair enough, creyshaw. You can handover the Storyteller now.'

"'No,' I said, although not very convincingly.

"He rolled his dead eyes. 'You creyshaws are all the same. You really must do something about this obnoxious need to display useless heroism. You're friend Anuenue went to the trouble of setting you up, you could at least be courteous enough to hand over the Storyteller and come with us back to Délon City without incident.'

"I looked at the multi-colored baboon. 'You little rat.'

"The large mandrill roared and leapt on Bobby's back. I grabbed the monkey by the scruff of its neck and flung it to the ground. It tumbled head over ass and then regained it's footing.

"'Enough!' General Roy shouted. He signaled for one of his soldiers to step forward and said something to him that I couldn't hear. The Délon he called forward steps back behind the tree line and re-emerges dragging a man dressed in silver armor by his arms. 'You can stop looking for your Keeper,' General Roy said. 'We've found him for you.'

"My knees began to shake. I was in way over my head. I had no idea what to do. I turned to Bobby to try to give him some words of comfort and was struck by the huge smile on his face. I suddenly realized he had read this story before.

"'Bobby,' I said, 'are we back on track. Is this the way the story is supposed to go?'

"'Almost,' he said.

"'Are you telling me there's a way out of this?' I asked.

"He nodded.

"'Help me out here, Bobby. What do I do?'

"A strong wind blew through the trees.

"'It's getting cold,' Bobby said hugging himself.

"'That's the least of our worries right now, Bobby,' I said.

"He pointed to General Roy who somehow looked less imposing. 'They don't like the cold.'

"'Great, but how does that help us?'

"Thunder crashed overhead. A flash of lighting shot through the sky.

"'It's going to start raining,' Bobby said.

"'You know, Bobby, I really appreciate these little weather reports, but if you want me to be totally honest they aren't really helping.'

"A rain drop hit my shoulder and then my nose. The water was cold... almost ice cold. I wiped the droplet from nose and rubbed it into my fingers. 'Freezing rain,' I said to no one in particular.

"A shriek came from General Roy's soldiers, followed by two more. General Roy mounted his horse, took one last look at us, and vanished into the tree line just as a steady rain began to fall.

"'Délons don't like the cold,' Bobby repeated.

"'Yeah,' I said. 'That was great timing.'

"The man dressed in armor was still face down where the Délon had dropped him. Kavi, Bobby, and I ran to him and turned him over. He was alive but he didn't speak. The armor helmet kept his face hidden. I struggled to remove it and when I finally did, I wanted to put it back on him as quickly as possible.

"The man in armor wasn't a man at all. His face was mostly teeth. His eyes and nose were barely visible. His grayish-green skin was slimy and pitted.

"'Wow,' I said to Bobby. 'You Storytellers are twisted.'

"'He's a Myrmidon,' he said.

"'And is that Latin for ugly?'

"'No,' Bobby said. 'It's American. Myrmidon's are ant people. They lived a long time ago. Some kind of god made them. Dr. Bashir told me about them. I thought they were neat.'

"'So if this is your Keeper, where are the monsters... Destroyers... whatever you call them?'

"'They can't come out until I'm captured. Those are the rules. Right now they're still people.'

"'Will they look like this?' I asked.

"'Yeah, 'cept they'll have black armor and they'll be a bunch of them.'

"'Do these people know they are the Myrmidons?'

"Bobby shook his head. 'I don't think so otherwise they would have never let me go.'

"'Let you go?'

"'Or tied me to the post so the lung locusts could get me.'

"Time seemed to stop as I processed Bobby's last statement. Carl and his community were the Myrmidons. Or they will be if the Destroyers get their hands on Bobby. I leaned in and studied the Keeper. I was trying to determine how critical he was when he convulsed and hacked up a thick glob of blood that struck me in the face. I jerked back. I screamed and frantically wiped the slick substance from my cheek.

"'He doesn't look too good,' Bobby said.

"With one eye closed to protect it from the Myrmidon's bloody discharge, I said, 'We should get him out of the rain.'

"I draped his arm over my shoulder and only then realized how large the Myrmidon actually was. I wouldn't be able to carry him very far. I dug my feet into the slippery mountainside and headed back to the path that had brought us this far. I had forgotten about Anuenue, and only thought about him when I wished there were more of us in our group. No surprise, he had vacated the area without a trace. He was a hunted baboon. As soon as the other apes got wind of his betrayal, they wouldn't stop until they found him, and when they found him, they wouldn't leave much of him behind.

"'Kavi,' I said dragging the Keeper. 'Find us a place to get out of the rain.'

"She extended her right index finger with her palm down and her other fingers pointing towards her. She made a large counterclockwise semi-circle around her left hand in the shape of a 'C.'

"Frustrated, I said, 'I don't understand.'

"She rolled her eyes and huffed.

"'You lead. We'll follow,' I said motioning with my head.

"She turned, quickly knuckle-walked to the other side of the path, and zipped through the foliage.

"'Slower!' I shouted as I struggled to drag the Myrmidon and keep pace with her. 'Bobby, run up there and tell her that I can't keep up with her.'

"'Okay,' Bobby said and then bolted past me. As soon as he was under the canopy of trees where Kavi had vanished, I lost sight of him.

'Bobby!' I said breathing heavy. 'Wait. Stay where I can see you.' He didn't answer. I stood on the edge of the tree line and shouted for Bobby and Kavi. I entered the darkness and almost immediately lost my bearings. It was impossibly dark. I could barely see two feet in front of me. I heard the ferns on the forest floor rustle and snap as I ventured further in. The Myrmidon's feet skidded and popped across the countless exposed tree roots that made it difficult to take more than one cautious step at a time. The ground dipped down and I stumbled into a churning creek. The bed was made up of loose gravel and mud. I trudged on, cursing myself for letting Bobby out of my sight. My knees began to shake and wobble. I couldn't go on much farther. I stopped to catch my breath. I was wet, scared, and exhausted. I thought of dropping the Myrmidon and coming back for him when I found Kavi and Bobby, but a mist had moved in and I knew with such poor visibility, I would never be able to find the Keeper again. I heard the howl of a chimpanzee just ahead. As I felt a wave of relief take over my body and give me a sudden burst of energy, I realized that what I thought was a chimpanzee howl could have just as well have been a mandrill howl. I put the thought out of my mind and stomped forward.

"A hand grabbed me out of the darkness and pulled me forward. Through the darkness I could make out the facial features of Kavi. She guided me through the mist and gloom until I heard Bobby's voice.

"'I told her,' he said. 'She didn't listen, but I told her.'

"Kavi helped me lay the Myrmidon gently on the side of the creek bed. 'You did good, Bobby. You did good.' I collapsed to the ground and sucked in as much oxygen as I could. To Kavi, 'Next time I'll lead and you carry the freakishly heavy ant man.'

"She flashed me a grin.

"I soaked in our surroundings. I could hear the rain pounding the treetops, but I couldn't feel the rain hitting us or the ground. The mist rolled and slowly drifted out of my line of sight. I noticed for the first time that there was a roof over our heads and walls to the right and left of us. I stood and placed my hand on the right wall. Rock. The same with the roof and the left wall. I looked at Kavi and repeated the sign she had given me earlier. 'Does this mean cave?'

"She pursed her lips and shrugged her shoulders as if to say 'Kind of.'

"I turned and looked into the mouth of the cave. I was about to meet the one and only Oz.

Oz

FOURTEEN

MIL STO. The letters look so big on the page they divert my attention from Scoop-face's session. MIL STO. The 'E' seemingly grew larger than the other letters. I move it in front of the MIL. EMILY. Lou's real first name is Emily. I can see her now in my mind's eye. We were standing in the charred Taker universe. She was walking away with Wes.

"Wait a minute," I said.

They stopped.

"Lou, what's your real name?"

She turned to me, tears in her eyes. "Emily," she said. "Emily Bristol."

I frenziedly write the name in the notebook. It was her. I scramble to my feet. "Emily," I say out loud.

Something slams against the door. I hear the sound of air exiting a human body.

"What are you doing, Bones?" Chester's voice practically crashed through the heavy wood door.

A pained voice responds. "Nothing."

"What's wrong with you? Why do you keep looking at that door?" Chester demanded.

"Nothing."

Chester slams Bones against the door again. I place my hand on the handle and close my eyes. I exhale and pull the door open. Bones falls into the closet. Chester looms in the hallway.

"What are you doing in there?" He barks. He drags me out of the closet by my shirt collar.

"Let me go!" I shout.

He tosses me to the ground. "This area ain't part of the GP pass."

I scoot back. "Emily Bristol," I say.

He looks at me confused. "What?"

"I know Lou's real name."

"Who's Lou and why do I care?" he says stomping forward.

"Snarkel, Snapper, Momma, Jaws, Spot, Jumper, Hambone, Charlie Boy," I hear from over my shoulder. I turn to see Bones standing in the closet doorway with his eyes rolled back in his head.

"Don't start up, Bones," Chester says.

"Snarkel, Snapper, Momma, Jaws, Spot, Jumper, Hambone, Charlie Boy."

A growl comes from the closet.

"What the...?" Chester says. He looks past Bones. Another growl. He steps forward. A chorus of growls. Chester leans in the open doorway. I hear a bark and see Chester stumble back. Charlie Boy bursts through the door and knocks Chester to the floor. Snarkle, Snapper, Momma, Jaws, Spot, and Hambone follow. Chester squeals.

"Call them off," I say to Bones.

"Back!" Bones yells.

The dogs back away from Chester, but keep snarling. "What's going on? Where did these dogs come from?" Chester asks, almost hyperventilating.

"I got news for you, Chester," I say. "You're about to find out you're a butterfly."

"What?"

"Keep him here," I say to Bones.

He nods with a maniacal smile on his face.

I run down the hallway to Dr. Graham's office and burst through the door. The doctor turns and stands. He's angry at first and quickly becomes frightened when he sees me.

"Oz... What...?"

"Emily Bristol..." I shout. "Her name is Emily Bristol!" Scoop-face sits up, a smile spreads across his eyeless and noseless face.

"What is this all about?" Dr. Graham asks.

"This is about the end of this nonsense," Scoop-face responds. "What do we do now?" I ask Scoop-face.

"Doc here sends us back," He says.

"See here," Dr. Graham interrupts. "I don't know what you're up to, but I'm going to have to insist you leave, Oz. Archie and I are in the middle..." He stops a confused look on his face. "We are in the middle of..."

"You're feeling it, aren't you, Doc?"

He looks at Scoop-face, "What...? I'm feeling a little disoriented..."

"Say her name again, kid," Scoop-face says to me.

"Emily Bristol."

Dr. Graham falls to his chair. He gasps and puts his hand over his mouth. "I... I... I know that name."

"What's happening?" I ask.

"You spoke her name," Scoop-face says. "You are creyshaw. The doc's starting to see that now."

"Because I spoke Lou's real name?"

"The Storytellers gave you this way out, Oz, so you could get back to where you belong, but you have to realize what you are. You're the key. That hasn't changed since day one. The Destroyers win if you're not in the fight. That day in the Georgia Dome when Ajax killed

Pepper, you made a deal with the Délons, if they let your friends go, you would help them find the Source. They agreed and, when you couldn't deliver on your promise, they locked you up here. Only here isn't here. It's here," he pointed to his head. "The Doc, Chester, the others, none of them are real." He blindly motions to Dr. Graham. "Ain't that right, doc?"

Dr. Graham slowly nods.

"What about you? Are you real?" I ask.

"Me? Yeah. Who would make this face up? He stands. "The Storytellers gave you an out, a magic word to get you back. You had to speak the real name of your one true love."

"True love?" I say indignantly. "I don't love Lou."

He snickers. "Sure... whatever. The important thing is you spoke her name and now Dr. Graham is forced to send us back."

"Where's back?" I ask.

"The cave. To the time we first met. The only way this works is if we go back without leaving here. If the Délons know we're not here, we lose the advantage."

I try to wrap my head around what he just said. "How do we go back and stay here?"

He extends his hand and searches for Dr. Graham. "That's where Doc comes in." He signals for me to come to the couch. "C'mon, let's do this."

I hesitate and then trot to the couch. I stop before I sit. "Wait a minute. What about Bones?"

"Bones can't go back."

"But he helped me."

"There's no place for him back there."

I scrutinize his face. "He's not real."

"Not back there he's not. Only here."

202

My heart aches for Bones. I hear nails clicking on the linoleum. His dogs create a half circle around the couch. Bones enters the room with a forlorn look on his face. "We can't just leave him here," I say to Scoop-face.

Scoop-face reaches for me and grabs my wrist, "He belongs here." He pulls me down. "We have to do this now." I sit on the couch next to him. "Bones," he says. "You're in charge while we're gone. Got it?"

"I can't go?" he asks, disappointment in his voice.

"We can't do this without you and your dogs, skinny man. You understand? Your place is here. These are the sacrifices you have to make when you are creyshaw."

He gulps. "I am creyshaw?"

"You are," Scoop-face says.

Bones's disappointment turns to incredible pride in the blink of an eye. "I am creyshaw," he says. "I will not leave this room. We will watch over you."

Scoop-face leans back. "Do your thing, Doc."

"What's happening to me?" he says examining his hands. His face twitches and he ages 20 years and then just as quickly he is a kid of thirteen and then back to his original age.

"We don't belong here anymore," Scoop-face says. "Everything's gone haywire. We stay much longer this whole place is going to collapse in on itself."

Dr. Graham looks at me. "Is this real?"

I nod. "I... I think so."

"Doc, get to hypnotizing, will ya'?" Scoop-face says.

Dr. Graham murmurs to himself and then orders us to close our eyes. He takes us through a breathing exercise and then begins to count backwards from ten. Just as I am slipping into a deep sleep, Scoop-face grabs my hand.

"Kid," he says, "I know this old face of mine ain't much to look at, but promise me you won't do anything different. No matter how much I beg you, don't change what you do to my face."

"Why?"

"Because," he snickers, "I am creyshaw."

"You're feeling relaxed, completely at ease," Dr. Graham's hypnotic monotone voice drones on. "You're getting sleepy now. As you feel your self falling into a deep sleep, you find yourself back in the cave where you belong."

Back

FIFTEEN

I opened my eyes and struggled to breathe. My head felt as if somebody had driven a spike through it. I sat up and surveyed the doctor's office. I felt something sliding down my chest, and howled in horror when I saw a shunter crawling down my torso. I batted it to the floor. It hit the soft clay surface. That's when I realized I wasn't in Dr. Graham's office. I was in the Pure's cave.

"Holy crap," I heard someone say.

I turned to see Gordy staring at me.

"It's really you, ain't it?" he asked.

I reached up and touched my face. "I think so. How old am I?"

Gordy shrugged. "I don't know. Ain't you a couple months younger than me?"

I study his face. He was a chubby-cheeked kid of about fifteen. I pumped my fist in the air. "I am back." I jumped off the gurney. My legs were weak and my knees almost buckled before I caught my balance.

"Easy, now," Gordy said. "You've been getting your brain sucked for a long time." He reached out and grabbed my arm to steady me. "The old sour puss was pretty impressed. He said he ain't never seen anyone survive as long as you did."

"Sour puss?"

"The Pure," Gordy said. "He did something to that shunter so it wouldn't never turn you Délon. It just tinkered with your brain. You remember anything at all?" he asked.

"Nothing I want to talk about," I said. I looked around the cave. "Where is our lovely host?"

"Headed toward the opening," Gordy said nodding his head to the right. "He heard a noise."

"Noise..." I said. "Scoop-face!" I stepped away from the gurney and tumbled to the ground. I was covered in clay.

"Scoop what?" Gordy said helping me to my feet.

"A friend of mine," I said out of breath. I regained my feet and placed my hands on my knees. "He was that noise."

"Oh," Gordy said. "Ewww, that's not good. Purey-boy don't like visitors. He turned the last guy inside out."

There was a minute of uncomfortable silence as I absorbed the information.

"You understand I mean that literally, right," Gordy said.

"I suspected as much," I said stumbling through the mud floor on weakened legs.

I saw Gordy duck his head and drop his chin to his chest. "What's wrong?"

"You picked up where you left off," he said. "You're bound and determined to do this hero thing. You know that is really kind of annoying."

"You going to help me or not?" I asked.

"Of course I'm going to help you. I'm the plucky sidekick." He put my arm around his shoulder. "Besides at the rate you're going, you'll never get there on your own."

With that, he helped me navigate the twists and turns of the cave until we could see beams of light bouncing off the rock walls. I looked ahead and saw what looked like the silhouettes of two men (or boys) and an ape. They were tending to another man on the ground. The Pure was nowhere to be seen. "Scoop-face... ahhh... Archie," I yelled.

The three silhouettes peered down the cave. I can hear them chatting, but it is nothing more than muttering from my vantage point. I step forward and see something moving to my immediate right. I nearly jump out of my skin when I see two white eyes staring back at me. The twisted figure of The Pure stepped forward.

He leaned in. "This isn't possible," he hissed.

I leaned back. "What's not possible?"

"You. This. You can't be awake. How are you able to walk... to stand... to breathe? I have not released you."

"Who's there?" I heard Archie yell.

"Stay there, Archie," I said.

"This is a trick," The Pure said.

"No trick," I said. "I'm here, and I'm staying this time." "Who's there?" Archie called out again.

"Stay there!" I shouted.

"Let them enter," The Pure groans. He sniffs. "The small one's blood smells so sweet."

"I know the Source," I said.

The Pure shifted his gaze from the mouth of the cave to me. "You lie."

"It's the truth."

His head bobbed nervously as he considered every inch of me. Looking for some sign I was lying. "What is it?"

I smiled. "We're not there yet. I have some conditions."

He wrapped his hand around my throat and shoved me up against the cave wall. I felt the blood racing through my veins.

"You waste my time with these lies," he growled.

I wheezed. "It's a picture." My body began to warm from the raging river of blood that was flowing through my veins.

"Easy, spidey-do," Gordy said. "If he's telling the truth, it would be the bonehead move of the century to kill him before he has a chance to tell you about this picture."

The Pure contemplated Gordy's logic. He released me and let me fall to the ground. "What of this picture?"

I massaged my bruised throat. "I know where it is. Your shunter must have jarred something lose in my memory banks because I know this picture exists. I've seen it. I know it's the Source the same as I know up is up and down is down."

"Where is it?"

"Oh, no," I said standing with Gordy's help. "I'm going to keep that to myself for a while."

The Pure reached for me, and I slapped his hand away. My blood was searing. He snarled and flared his mandibles. I pushed him to the cave floor. He landed on his back with a thud.

"Whoa," Gordy said. "What are doing...? How are you doing that?"

I opened and closed my hand creating a tighter and tighter grip with each flex. "The shunter must have done something to me."

The Pure crawled up the cave wall like an insect and hid himself in a dark crevice.

"Listen to me," I said. "I'll bring you your picture, but you've got to give me something in return."

I heard him snivel. "Watch your tongue, boy. Your strength is temporary. You'll be weak and useless soon enough."

I examined the back of my hand. "Maybe, but I don't think so. I got this weird feeling that you turned something on in my brain you shouldn't have. Funny thing is..." I reached up in the darkness toward the sound of his voice, found the collar of his ragged shirt and yanked him out of his hiding place. He flopped to the ground. "I think you know it, too."

"Ozzie, boy," Gordy said. "I think you better cool off. I seen the old Pure here do some pretty ugly stuff while you was taking your shunter-faced nap."

I turned to him. "Just what is your role in all this, Gordy?" He held up his hand. "Easy now. Easy. I'm your compadre. Your number one best friend."

I lurched forward. "Friend? You live with this slime, how can you be my friend?"

"It was part of the deal."

I pushed him backward. He stumbled on the loose gravel of the cave floor. "Deal?"

"General Roy was sucking the life out of you, man."

I pushed him again. The sound of his voice felt as though it was stabbing my eardrums. I was growing angrier the more he talked.

"He was going to kill you to get what he wanted. I couldn't let that happen. So, we made a deal." He backed away from me grabbing in the darkness for the cave wall.

"What deal? Who's we?"

He shifted his eyes from me to behind me. "She's we."

I turned to see General Roy's sister standing behind me. "Reya?"

She stepped forward, dead-eyes locked on mine, her spider-leg hair flailing madly. She sniffed the air. "Still alive. How disappointing."

Still enraged, I rushed her. She swiftly stepped out of the way, and I rammed my head into the cave wall. I dropped to the ground.

"Hey, not cool," Gordy shouted. "Not cool." He raced

to my side.

I rolled over on my back. My head felt like a cracked egg. My anger was replaced with excruciating pain. "What deal?" I moaned.

"I found The Pure. I made a deal with him. If I brought him to you, he would get you to reveal the Source without torturing you like General Roy was. I couldn't get to you. So I went to her. She helped me get you to The Pure."

I sat up with great difficulty. "Why would she do that?"

"General Roy is weak," she screeched. "He's disgraced the Délons. I aligned myself with the Pure to save my kind."

I chuckled. "You're not doing this for your kind."

The Pure hobbled forward. "He knows you well, my queen."

I smiled. "Now it makes sense." I stood with Gordy's help. "Wait a minute. I was in... that place... Scoop-face said the Délons put me there... I'm still there... on the couch... Bones is watching over us."

"The Délons put you there, but I've kept you there," the Pure said. "It was necessary to keep General Roy at bay."

Reya smiled. "The one called Bones is my cow. He is our decoy. He lays on a table in Délon City in your stead. His brain's being fed upon by a royal shunter. He is most likely dead by now, but he is just a cow."

I grunted. Stepping forward I fought to suppress the anger that had engulfed me earlier. "He is creyshaw," I said to Reya.

She took some satisfaction in my tone. She had gotten to me.

"What about Canter? He's been helping Lou and the others."

"Helping?" Reya laughed. "He works for General Roy. He hasn't been helping them. He's been using them."

"Why?"

"They've long felt the Lou knew of the Source, too. They had hopes that eventually she would lead them to it. She's proven to be a great disappointment."

I moved down the cave toward the entrance. "I don't completely understand what's going on here, but I'm back, and I'm calling the shots now. You want the Source you play my way."

The Pure crawled along the cave wall in pursuit of me. "I won't be ordered around by a human..."

"Then kiss the Source goodbye."

Furious, he groaned like a wounded animal.

"Control your human," Reya barked at The Pure.

He roared. "I cannot."

"Fine, then I shall do your job for you," she said. I turned to her when I heard the sound of Gordy gasping for air. Her hand was clamped around his neck. "I will snap your guardian's skinny neck," she said.

I smiled. "Go ahead. I'll just burn the Source."

"Fine," she growled. "Destroy it. Better no one have it than let it fall in the hands of General Roy."

"You would have killed me a long time ago if that's what you really thought."

She jerked her hand away from Gordy's neck and tossed him toward me. "I am watching you. You betray us, and I will kill him and the girl and the fat one."

I caught Gordy before he hit the ground. "I'll bring you the Source when it's time and not one second before." Gordy and I headed for the mouth of the cave. "So you were my guardian?"

He nodded massaging his throat. "You think I was going to trust that Pure puke to keep his word? You made a deal. I had to make sure he kept his end of the bargain."

"Yeah?" I said. "I guess that's pretty cool."

"You guess?" he said sounding offended.

I lightly pushed him as we walked. It was all the thanks I was up to giving at the moment. I hoped he understood.

As we got closer to the cave opening, the details of the people who had just been silhouettes began to fill in. I saw Little Bobby's face first. It was drawn and pale. Mud covered most of his forehead. He bore a hopeful grin as Gordy, and I approached.

Kavi sat with her feet underneath her. She let out a guttural whoop as we got closer. The hair on her shoulders stood on end.

Scoop-face stood to her right only he was not Scoop-face. Not there. Not in that time. He was Archie Maynard. Young, fresh-faced, alive in a way I could not have imagined when we first met in the hallway of the "facility." He stared at me in confused wonder. I picked apart every detail of his eyes. They were green with specs of gold. His nose was strong and prominent. What my mother would have called a Roman nose. He was not at all what I pictured him to be. He was a few inches taller than me now. "Hello," I said.

Archie looked at Kavi. The chimp was growing increasingly agitated. "He's okay," he said turning back to me. "I think."

"You know this guy?" Gordy asked.

"We've met," I said.

"We have?" Archie asked.

I stuck out my hand and noticed for the first time that my arm was now covered in fine light hairs. The dark bushy forearm I had sported just a few minutes ago was completely gone. "My name is Oz Griffin, and I am creyshaw."

Archie hesitated and then shook my hand. "I... I am creyshaw, too. Archie..."

"Maynard," I said. "The warrior with two hearts."

He looked at me cock-eyed and stepped back. "What's going on?"

"I'm Gordy in case anyone cares," Gordy said.

"You don't remember anything?" I asked.

"What are you talking about?" Archie asked.

I thought about explaining everything to him, but I quickly decided against it. We didn't have the time for me to try to convince him that he was in two places at once. I wasn't even sure I believed it.

A pained squeak shot up from the ground. It was then I noticed the Myrmidon Keeper laying next to Kavi. "How is he," I asked.

"I don't know," Archie shrugged. "How do you know how a ant-guy... man... person... is really doing? This could be normal for him... it, for all I know."

I squatted down next to the Keeper. "This doesn't look normal," I said examining the Myrmidon closer. "General Roy and his boys really did a number on him."

The Myrmidon coughed and spit up a bright yellow mucus.

"Nice," Gordy said.

"I'm not too sure he's going to make it," I said.

Archie knelt down next to me. "What happens if a keeper dies?"

"Not sure," I said. "How 'bout you, Bobby? You know what happens if a Keeper dies?"

"They come through," he answered. "Some of them, anyway. The rest come when the Délons catch me."

I stood. "Well, let's not get ahead of ourselves. This Myrmidon's not dead, and the creyshaw won't let the Délons get you."

Little Bobby hung his head. "That ain't how the story goes." A horse whinnied in the distance.

"Uh-oh," Gordy said. "I'm guessing that ain't the cavalry."

"I thought it was too cold for those guys," Archie said.

We heard the howl of a mandrill.

"That little..." Archie said.

I turned to look down the cave. I couldn't see a thing ten feet in. It was a dead end and would leave us cornered if we decide to use it as our refuge. There was only one thing left to do.

"Quick! Grab his feet," I instructed Gordy. He hesitated. "C'mon, now. You can complain later."

Sensing the urgency of the situation, Gordy did as requested and grabbed the Myrmidon's feet. I grabbed his hands. To Archie, "Lead the way!"

He hesitated.

"Today, Archibald," Gordy barked. "We're about to be up to our necks in purple pukes."

Archie turned in a panic and then stopped. By his stiff body language, I could tell he was going over an imaginary checklist in his mind. I could tell because I had done the same thing as a leader. He snapped his fingers and turned to Bobby. "Up here with me, Little B. You're still my responsibility."

We trudged along the creek bed. The almost superhuman strength I had experienced earlier was gone. I could barely lift the Myrmidon off the ground. Gordy wasn't faring any better. Tired of watching our pathetic attempt to carry the giant ant-man, Kavi pushed us aside and dragged the Myrmidon at a much faster pace than we could carry him.

We heard the sound of General Roy's men moving through the forest. The gloom hid their direction. We had no idea if we were traveling towards them or away from. Eventually we heard the sound of boots slogging through the water. They were in the creek bed, too.

Gordy whispered loudly, "This is crazy. We can't see where we're going."

"We're almost to the clearing," Archie answered.

"How do you know?' Gordy asked.

Archie hesitated. "Because we have to be."

"Human," General Roy's voice boomed through the darkness. "Give us the Storyteller!"

Archie suddenly stopped, and the rest of us crashed into him. His breathing was unsteady.

"Move," I said. "What are you doing?"

"I'm lost," Archie responded. "I got turned around." A dog barked.

"Did your hear that?" Archie asked.

I nodded not realizing that it was a useless response because no one could see me. The dog barked again. "Go," I said. "It's in front of us. Follow the sound of the bark."

Slowly we moved forward, adjusting our direction slightly with each subsequent bark. The dog was leading us out of the woods.

After several minutes, we reached the tree line and stepped into the clearing and stopped. We all looked over our shoulders to admire what we had escaped. I turned back and looked across the large expanse of the sloped clearing and thought I saw a ghostly stick-thin figure standing on the opposite side. He held a rambunctious dog by the collar. In the blink of an eye, Bones and Charlie boy were both gone.

Archie looked over the group and nodded confidently. Kavi let go of the Myrmidon long enough to sign to us impatiently. She wanted to keep moving and she made it emphatically clear.

We rushed across the clearing into a cold wind. I hoped it was enough to keep the Délons back. They were weakened. That was clear. It wasn't just the cold weather either. It was beyond that. Something was zapping them of their power. I didn't much care what it was. I just hoped it continued. By the time we reached the other side of the clearing, it was apparent they were no longer following us. It was more than likely just a temporary postponement of their pursuit, but it was all we needed for now.

***

We must have been a mile from the camp when we heard the first screech in the gloomy sky above us. It was an inhuman screech. I guessed it to be a gibbon. I had seen something about them on Animal Planet when the world was normal. The warbling howl that surrounded us at that moment sounded just like the gibbons on that program. It was a distress call. Another howl soared above us, followed by a deafening roar. I heard a man scream. The battle between Carl's crew and the apes was in full swing. I pushed ahead to the front of the line. I turned to the others and signaled them to stop.

"This is where you get off," I said to Archie.

"What?" he asked, shocked and confused. "No! No way! I've got some unfinished business in there."

"You've got unfinished business here," I said. I motioned to Bobby.

"I did my part," he barked, stepping toward me with bad intentions. "I got him to his Keeper. I can't help it if the Keeper is half-dead."

"We've still got a chance as long as Bobby's alive and he's under our care," I said. "I'm not the smartest guy in the world, but even I can figure out walking him into a war zone is no way to secure his safety. You, Kavi, Bobby, and the Myrmidon need to get as far away from this place as possible. I suggest you loop around the fight and look for higher elevation. The colder it is the better. The Délons won't be able to get to you."

"Hey, boss," Gordy said. "Any chance I can get out of this fight?"

"I'm afraid you're stuck with me," I said.

"Hold on!" Archie shouted. "This isn't settled. I know you're supposed to be this super warrior, Oz, but all I see is some scrawny kid who likes to order people around."

Gordy said. "You can get pretty bossy, Oz-man."

"You're not helping," I said to Gordy. I pulled Archie aside. "I know you want to make Carl pay for what he did to Tank. I don't blame you, but there are more important things to consider here..."

"Wait a minute," he said. "How do you know about Tank?"

"We don't have time to go into that right now. Let's just say I know a lot of things. I know about Tank. I know you hate the song "Friends in Low Places," because it's the only song Bobby knows and he won't stop singing it. I know you saved April from the halfer. I know a lot of things. And you have to trust me that I know that taking Bobby any closer to the fight in front of us is the worst move you can make."

He looked at me dumbfounded. He wrung his hands together, and grunted as he began to speak, only to stop abruptly because he had no idea what to say. Finally, he groaned, "Damn it!"

I smiled and nodded.

A pained squeal soared through the night air. Kavi hooted. She knew the ape the squeal came from. She leaned forward and then forced herself to back away. She wanted to join the fight, too.

"The Storytellers are all that matter in this world," I said. "We do whatever it takes to keep them safe. Understood?"

Archie stared at me for a long time. He sighed heavily and then turned to Bobby. "Let's go, Little B." They turned to the right and took a parallel path back up the slope. Gordy and I helped Kavi hoist the Myrmidon on her back and watched her lumber after her human companions. Just as the small band of travelers was about to disappear into a thick row of hemlock trees, Archie stopped and shouted. "I am creyshaw!"

Gordy shook his head. "Nice. He should yell a little louder so every creepy crawly on the mountain knows where to find him." I smiled. "He is creyshaw, Gordy."

He shrugged. "So. What does that mean?"

"That means I feel sorry for any creepy crawly that does find him."

SIXTEEN

We found a dead gorilla with an arrow through his neck shortly after Gordy and I split from the others. It was a young male. Ten feet from the gorilla we found the twisted body of some teenage boy. The kid was dressed in black from head to toe. A member of Carl's crew, no doubt. A orangutan was huddled next to the dead boy. It was trembling. It didn't take notice of us until we were mere feet away. The orange ape turned, flashed a toothy grimace, but didn't advance.

I slowly put my hands up in front of me. "It's okay." The orangutan pounded a fist on the ground and barked. "We are on you side, red," Gordy said.

The ape grabbed the twisted body of the boy and cradled it. "What do you make of that?" Gordy asked.

I shook my head. "I don't know. I think he's confused. He's been taught to protect humans, and now he's forced to fight them."

We carefully made our away around the orangutan and the boy and moved closer to the battle that was raging on in front of us. The groans, growls, hoots, and screams grew more and more intense as we inched forward. The instinct to flee was growing nearly impossible to fight. One look into Gordy's eyes and I could see he was struggling with the same impulses.

"Tell me this is a good idea," he whispered.

"This is a good idea," I said with no feeling at all.

He snickered. "You're a terrible liar."

As I was about to comment, I was interrupted by a hriek of unbelievable power and volume. A brown blur leapt from a nearby tree and knocked Gordy to the ground. I sprang forward only to have my left ankle whacked by a heavy tree limb. I crumpled in pain and flailed on the forest floor trying to rub the burning sensation out of my leg. A chimp's face emerged in my line of sight. I quickly adjusted to the shock of seeing the ape suddenly appear, and determined that it was holding a rock above its head. It was about to bash my brains in.

"Hey!" a voice boomed. "Get your furry ass away from there!" The chimp looked up, huffed, and then backed away.

I peered up and nearly burst into tears when I saw Wes's fat frame plodding toward me. I immediately forgot about the pain in my ankle and stood up. "Wes!"

"I'll be a monkey's uncle," he said as he approached. He put his hands on my shoulders and looked at me carefully. "Is it really you, Oz?"

"I think it is," I said.

He guffawed. "Lordy! Lordy! Lordy!" he said hugging me so tight I could barely breathe.

We heard a screech and wail, followed by Gordy screaming, "Get this thing off me!"

Wes and I couldn't help but laugh as we watched Gordy trying to fight off a small spider monkey.

"Did you have to bring him?" Wes asked.

Gordy successfully knocked the tiny primate from his shoulder and struggled to catch his breath. "Nice to see you too, Wes!"

"Come here," Wes said putting his burly arm around Gordy and pulling him in for a bear hug.

The wisp of an arrow flying through the forest and the

whack of the arrow hitting a nearby tree put a sudden end to our happy reunion. We all dropped to the ground and took cover.

"Man," Wes grunted. "Those little punks brought the firepower with them."

"How many are there?" I asked.

"Hard to tell," Wes said. "I'm guessing three dozen or so. But as well trained as they are, there might as well be a couple of hundred of them."

"What weapons do we have?"

"Four crossbows, some knives... nothing compared to what they've got."

"I'm for turning around," Gordy said.

"Where's..." I hesitated before I said her name. I was almost afraid of Wes's answer. "Lou?"

"We split up when this whole thing started. She spotted some poor sucker with J.J. and took off. She ain't the most rational person."

"That's what makes her a great warrior," I said smiling.

I looked through the thicket of trees to try to get a handle of the state of the battle. I spotted a silverback squared off against six of Carl's crew, half armed with bows and arrows, the other half armed with large hunting knives. I caught a glimpse of the silverback's scarred face and recognized Ajax's snarl. I bolted ahead without a word to Wes and Gordy.

"Hey," Wes growled. "What in tarnation do you think you're doing?"

I felt a few arrows fly by my head as I raced through the woods. The searing heat of anger was coursing through my blood. I felt a surge of strength rise up inside of me. Previous experience with this phenomenon suggested the feeling was fleeting and wouldn't last long. I had to take advantage of it quickly. I leapt through the air and tackled one of Ajax's attackers to the ground. The arrow he had cocked flew harmlessly into the treetops. One of his friends tried to react quickly to my attack with a swift kick aimed at my head. I ducked, and the booted foot landed squarely on the jaw of the kid I had just tackled. I jumped to my feet and pushed the first body I could find into the next body. It was total chaos. Ajax grunted, and I heard the glorious pock, pock, pock of him pounding his chest. I was back with my warriors. I was where I belonged.

Ajax had taken out four of the Carl's crew before the other two bolted through the woods and out of sight. I turned to my old gorilla friend and shrugged, "You're slipping, old friend. You used to be the one who came to my rescue."

Ajax hooted. He teetered forward on two legs. His brown eyes nearly sucked the life out of me he was peering at me so intensely.

"It's me," I said. "It's really me."

He grabbed me and put me in a bear hug that dwarfed Wes's. I patted his massive back. "Easy, big guy," I wheezed. "Easy."

"Let him go, you big ape," Wes barked. "You're going to smother him to death."

Ajax released me. He bobbed his head while letting out a rapid-fire series of yowls.

"Lord goodness almighty Aphrodite, I ain't never seen him carry on like that," Wes said

"Hey, fellas," Gordy said. "I hate to rain on this love fest, but you do know that there are a bunch of guys dressed in black running around here carrying lots of pointy things, right?"

The words had just settled on our eardrums when Gordy yelped and grabbed his shoulder. The arrow that struck him had splintered upon striking him. I turned to see a redheaded girl slowly approach with a bow loaded and cocked.

"Wait a minute, little miss," Wes said. "Wait a minute." Ajax panted.

"Madison," I said.

She stopped and lowered the arrow. "Do I know you?"

"No," I said. "But I know you. You helped Archie and the others."

She cocked her head as she studied me. "Where is he?"

I thought about the question. "Making up for some mistakes," I said. I stepped forward. She raised the arrow again. I saw a bruise under her right eye.

"Carl do that?" I ask.

She looked away for a split second and then turned her focus back on me. "Rules are rules," she said. "And consequences are consequences."

"And fathers are fathers."

She clenched her teeth. "How do you know so much about me?"

"Let's just say I heard some things."

"Look, miss," Wes said. "I'd really appreciate it if you'd just put that bow and arrow down. Ain't no harm happened here yet..."

"Excuse me," Gordy said holding his shoulder. "What about me?"

Wes frowned. "Okay, almost then. Ain't no real harm been done. You'll live."

Distracted by the exchange between Wes and Gordy, Madison didn't notice the baboon that had snuck up behind her. In the blink of an eye, it dashed forward and ripped the bow and arrow from Madison's grip. Gordy stumbled forward and tackled her to the ground. He raised a fist, and Wes immediately stepped in.

"Oh, no," Wes said grabbing Gordy by the forearm.

"Can't let you do that, my friend."

"She tried to kill me," Gordy screamed.

"No she didn't," I said. "You'd be dead if she was trying to kill you."

Gordy huffed. "I suppose you want me to thank her for shooting me in the shoulder."

"You don't have to thank me," Madison said. "Just get off me, and we'll call it even."

"Listen here," Gordy growled. "Don't get smart..." Madison grabbed Gordy's hair, and he let out a high-pitched shriek.

Wes and I pulled them apart chuckling madly as we did. We didn't hear Carl and his crew approach. It was the arrow that struck Wes in the leg that finally got our attention. I spun on my heels desperately trying to muster the anger that gave me superhuman strength. It never came. We were severely outnumbered, and they had a trump card that kept me in check. One of Carl's crew held my old sword J.J. to Lou's neck.

I felt a heavy pounding in my chest. I heard the thumping of my own heart. Every breath I took was amplified. My mouth went dry. She had changed since the last time I saw her, but I could still see that scared, dirt covered little girl I first saw in the Kroger's store in Manchester. Her eyes opened wide when she saw me. She wanted to run and wrap her arms around me, but she couldn't. She swallowed, and I could see tears forming in her eyes.

Carl saw it, too. "My, my, someone's happy to see you," he said to me.

"Let her go," I said.

"Hmm," he said. "Let me think about it... Ahhh, no. You're all coming with us."

Ajax roared, charged forward, and wrapped his huge

leathery hand around Madison's neck. She fruitlessly slapped at his arm.

It was clear he had reduced her ability to breathe. She had to gasp to catch a breath.

Carl motioned for two of his crew to move in. Ajax responded by increasing pressure on Madison's neck.

"Ajax," I said. "Don't..."

"Break her neck," Wes said wincing in pain.

"What? No!" I snapped.

Lou yelped in pain as the kid holding the sword to her pressed harder and pierced the skin on her neck. Blood trickled down the blade.

"Stop!" I demanded.

"Kill her," Carl said to Ajax. "Snap her neck like a twig. She's been a terrible disappointment anyway. I'll of course order Jerry to slice this one's neck open." He circled Lou as he talked. "It's a shame, too. She's a real fighter. If I had known, I wouldn't have tried to sacrifice her to the lung locusts."

"Mister," Wes wheezed. "You kill that little one, and I promise you I will tear you limb from limb, put you back together, and do it all over again."

"Nobody is going to kill anybody," I said. "We'll turn Madison over to you and you're going to turn Lou back over to us."

"Forgive me," Carl sneered. "but this isn't a negotiation. Either you're all coming with us, or you're all going to die."

I scowled and stepped forward. "Carl, I don't really like you." He wrinkled his brow. "Do I know you?"

I shook my head. "No, but I know you. I know where your complex is. I know Madison is your daughter. I know you like to bully kids into believing that you're this great leader when the truth is you couldn't lead a Boy Scout troop in a sing-along. You're as phony as a silk flower."

He cleared his throat and stuck his chin out in an effort to look more authoritative. "Kill them," he said to Jerry.

"Whoa," Gordy said holding his wounded shoulder. "Let's not do anything rash. Oz has been out of the loop for a while. He's not really feeling like himself. So let's just relax. Maybe we should just sit down and get to know each other. I'm a Libra..."

"Shut up, boy," Wes said.

Ajax narrowed his glaring eyes and dragged Madison forward. Jerry raised his arrow. "The ape..."

"What about him?" Carl barked.

"He'll kill Maddy as soon as I fire."

"Did I ask you to access the situation, soldier?"

"No, sir," Jerry responded.

"What I did I order you to do?"

"Kill them, sir."

"Then what is the problem?"

Sweat formed on Jerry's face. "She's your daughter..."

Carl raised his crossbow and fired. The arrow struck Madison in the chest with a sickening thud. Startled, Ajax released his death grip on her neck and gently cradled her head in the crook of his arm.

A deafening silence shattered the anger and tension that had been building. Carl's crew stood in stunned disbelief. In an instant, Carl had changed from leader to monster.

"Kill them!" he screamed.

Wes fumed. "Two minutes, pal! That's all I want. Two minutes alone with you!"

I knelt next to Ajax. Madison was alive, but barely. Blood was coming out of her mouth. She struggled to breathe. She looked at me with a blank stare. "I miss my mom."

"It's okay," I said.

She swallowed. "It doesn't hurt that much."

"Shut her up!" Carl screamed.

She laughed and then winced in pain. "He destroyed himself." With that, she took one last breath.

"What did she mean by that?" Carl asked. "I didn't destroy myself. I'm right here. I'm a god! Nothing can destroy me!"

I stood and approached Carl. His eyes were as blank as his daughter's. She was right. He did destroy himself. I yanked the crossbow from his hand. I addressed his crew. "This is over."

A quick scan of the perimeter revealed dozens of ape eyes staring back at us.

Jerry pointed his arrow at me. "He did what he had to. She was weak."

I pushed the arrow down. "It's over. You can come with us, or you can go back to your complex. It's up to you."

Carl dropped to his knees. He began to wail. "I am a god!"

The ground suddenly shook beneath our feet. A belch of stale air rolled through the forest. I stuck my hands out to balance myself. Most of Carl's crew tumbled to the ground. The apes screeched as the earth trembled.

Carl screamed, "I'm on fire!" His skin began to drop off in chunks. His bones cracked and snapped as his body grew in every direction. One-by-one, the same thing happened to everyone in his crew.

Gordy yelped in astonished horror. Wes groaned, and Ajax yowled in disbelief. Lou was so shocked she couldn't move. She stood among the crippled crew and watched them morph into Myrmidons.

"Lou!" I shouted in order to be heard over the sounds

of Carl's crew screaming. She couldn't hear me. I ran to her. "Lou."

She looked up. It took a second or two for her to register what was going on, who I was, and what she was doing standing in the middle of human bodies literally being split apart.

She wrapped her arms around my neck and whispered "You're not leaving me again." I pulled her out of the flailing mass of people... or what were once people.

Wes limped to us. "What in tarnation..."

"Damn it!" Gordy yelled, "He didn't make it!"

"Who didn't make it?" Wes asked.

"We don't have time to discuss this," I said. "We need to get as far away from here as we quickly as we possibly can."

We maneuvered through the trees and headed down the mountain. Wes sucked in air with each step. The arrow was still protruding from his leg. He hobbled along stopping briefly every other step in order to muster up the strength to take another jolt of pain. As he planted his foot in the loose dirt and one more shot of agony soaked every nerve in his body, a thought came to him. "Wait! Where's Ty and April?"

We all looked at each other. Gordy finally spoke up. "Who's April?"

"A girl we picked up outside of Edisto," Wes said. "She and Ty were together just before this whole mess started." "What about Valerie?" Gordy asked. "Where is she?"

Wes and Lou traded a look. Neither one of them wanted to answer Gordy's question so they simply didn't.

Wes turned to head back up the slope.

"Where are you going?" I asked.

"I ain't leaving Ty. I'm tired of losing people."

He took one step and nearly flopped to the ground in pain. "I'd say that's not going to happen," I said. I called Ajax over.

I held up two fingers. "Pick two apes to find Tyrone and April." He grunted and barreled across the fern-covered ground. He stopped on the edge of a small clearing and signed to a much larger silverback that I assumed was Ariabod. Ariabod in turn signaled to a young male gorilla to his left. They looked our way and then disappeared into the nearby bush.

"So help me," Wes said breathing heavily. "Those monkeys better bring them back alive."

"They will," I said. "And they're not monkeys..." Out of the corner of my eye, I caught Lou staring at me. "What?" I asked her.

"Are you real?" she asked.

I smiled. "I wish I knew."

Gordy piped up. "Any idea where we're going? And shouldn't we be getting the hell out of here? Or did you forget the giant ant people?"

I strained to stop looking at Lou. I was afraid if I let her out of my sight she would vanish into thin air. "Yeah... sure, you're right. Let's go!" I said and then stopped short when I saw a boy who had been one of the dead who watched me sleep at the facility. He was standing amid a group of sapling pine trees. Our eyes locked and then the boy turned and headed down the mountain.

"Okay," Gordy said. "I guess we won't be going that way."

"No," I said my eyes still locked on the boy. "I think we're supposed to."

"Oz," Gordy responded. "That kid was major stand-out-in-the-crowd-creepy, and that ain't easy to achieve in this place."

"I've seen him before," I said. "He's dead."

"Nice!" Gordy shouted. "Just exactly where is the dead kid taking us?"

Ajax rejoined us. He cupped his hands with the palms up, moved his thumbs across his fingers, and then turned his right palm down. He flipped the position of his hands. He repeated the signs a few times.

"What's he saying?" Wes asked.

"Don't know," I said.

Lou cleared her throat. "He's saying ... 'the land of the dead'."

The End
of
Book Three